Tiger
STONE

Tiger STONE

DERYN MANSELL

black dog books

First published in 2014
by ✂ black dog books,
an imprint of Walker Books Australia Pty Ltd
Locked Bag 22, Newtown
NSW 2042 Australia
www.walkerbooks.com.au

1

The moral rights of the author have been asserted.

Text © 2014 Deryn Mansell

All rights reserved. No part of this publication may be reproduced,
stored in a retrieval system, or transmitted in any form or by
any means – electronic, mechanical, photocopying, recording or
otherwise – without the prior written permission of the publisher.

National Library of Australia Cataloguing-in-Publication entry:
Mansell, Deryn, author.
Tiger stone / Deryn Mansell.
ISBN: 978 1 742032 39 9 (paperback)
For primary school age.
Subjects: Family secrets – Juvenile fiction.
Villages – Indonesia – Java – Juvenile fiction.
Java (Indonesia) – 14th century – Juvenile fiction.
A823.4

Cover (face) © Emmanuel R Lacoste/Shutterstock.com
Cover, pp 13, 19, 255 (tiger) © Apostrophe/Shutterstock.com
Cover, pp 6-7 (old paper background) © iStock.com/Eerik
Page 7 (torn paper banner) © iStock.com/robynmac
Typeset in Adobe Garamond Pro
Printed and bound in Great Britain by Clays Ltd, St Ives plc

For my parents, who introduced me to Java,
and Mrs Lien Lee, *seorang guru yang luar biasa*.

SUNDA KINGDOM

Muara
Jati

Pekalongan

✖ KAWALI
CAPITAL OF THE
SUNDA KINGDOM

✖ CENTRE OF POWER

• Town or village

O Mountain

— Kancil's sea journey

--- Kancil's overland journey

Mataram lands

JAVA
in the fourteenth century

MAJAPAHIT
KINGDOM

• Salatiga

Mbah
Merapi

• Prambanan

Bubat •
✗
TROWULAN
CAPITAL OF THE
MAJAPAHIT KINGDOM

CHARACTERS

Aryani (*ari-yani*): A modern-day girl from Java, Indonesia

Ma: Her mother

Bapak Surya (*bah-pahk sooh-ree-ya*): Their neighbour

Kancil (*kahn-chil*): A fourteenth-century girl from the Sunda Kingdom

Mother/Sumirah (*soo-mee-rah*): Kancil's mother from the Majapahit Kingdom

Father: Kancil's father from the Sunda Kingdom

Agus (*ah-goos*): Kancil's brother

Small Aunt/Ibu Jamu (*i-booh jah-moo*): Kancil's aunt (her mother's younger sister)

Big Uncle/Bapak Thani (*bah-pahk tah-nee*): Kancil's uncle (her mother's older brother)

Big Aunt/Ibu Thani (*i-booh tah-nee*): Big Uncle's wife

Citra (*chit-trah*): Kancil's cousin

Bibi (*bib-bee*): The cook

Ida (*i-dah*): A kitchen servant

Kitchen Boy: A kitchen servant

Ibu Tari (*i-booh tah-ree*): A village woman

Bapak Pohon (*bah-pahk poh-hon*): A village man (Ibu Tari's husband)

The *juru kunci* (*joo-roo khun-chee*): A village elder, responsible for communicating with the spirits

Ki Sardu (*ki sar-doo*): A village elder, the priest

Bapak Iya (*bah-pahk ee-yah*): A village elder

The prince/Bhre Mataram (*bray maht-arr-ahm*): A prince of the Majapahit Kingdom/Ruler of the Mataram lands

The parasol bearer, Itam (*i-tahm*), **Fatty**, **Scar**, **Tor** and **Red**: Servants of the prince

Dalang Mulyo (*dah-lahng moohl-yoh*): A puppet master

PLACES

Bubat: A place on the northern outskirts of the Majapahit capital, Trowulan.

Lawucilik: A village that might have existed somewhere in Java.

Majapahit Kingdom: A kingdom from the thirteenth to the sixteenth century. From its capital, Trowulan in eastern Java, the kingdom dominated much of South East Asia in the fourteenth century.

Mataram lands: An outlying region of the Majapahit Kingdom. During the first Mataram Kingdom (eighth to tenth century) many temples, including Prambanan, were built here. Little is known of the people who lived here in the fourteenth century but by the end of the sixteenth century it was again an important centre, this time for the second Mataram Kingdom.

Mbah Merapi: A mountain in the centre of Java and one of Indonesia's most active volcanoes (Mbah Merapi = Fiery Grandfather).

Muara Jati: A port on the north coast of the Sunda

Kingdom where modern-day Cirebon stands.

Nusantara: Literally "the islands between", this term originally referred to the islands outside Java. It is now used as an alternative name for Indonesia.

Pekalongan: A port on the north coast of central Java.

Prambanan: A village at the foot of Mount Merapi near where the Prambanan temple complex stands.

Salatiga: A mountain village in Java, north of Prambanan.

Sunda Kingdom: A kingdom in western Java from the seventh to the sixteenth century.

Trowulan: The capital city of the Majapahit Kingdom.

Yogyakarta: A city in the centre of Java, south of Mount Merapi. In the fourteenth century it was a part of the Mataram lands.

NOW

PROLOGUE

Aryani peered at herself in the bathroom mirror while she combed her fringe to cover her eyes. Ma said her teak-coloured eyes were pretty, and Grandma loved them of course – they reminded her of her son, who died less than a year after Aryani was born. Aryani didn't like drawing attention to herself so she hid her eyes from strangers.

It didn't matter so much in the village, where everybody knew her as the quiet girl with the big brain. Now that brain had won her a scholarship to a high school in the city. She had never left the village in her life and she was about to get on a bus to Yogyakarta where she would be surrounded by staring strangers.

The cardboard suitcase was packed and waiting on the verandah, where Ma was drinking tea with Bapak

Surya, the neighbour who would accompany Aryani to the boarding house in the city.

"Are you ready, Ani?" Ma called.

Aryani took a gulp of sweet tea from a glass in the kitchen. The cold tea helped to calm the sick feeling that was rising in her throat. "I'll just say goodbye to Grandma," she called back.

Why had she ever thought that going to high school in the city was a good idea? Ma didn't want her to go and none of the neighbours had anything good to say about the city. In fact, the only person who had encouraged her to go was Grandma. "Yogyakarta is not like other cities," she had said. "It's a place of learning."

Aryani squared her shoulders. She couldn't disappoint Grandma.

The room was dark and the smell of *kayu putih* oil hung in the air. "Is that my little Kancil?" Grandma said when Aryani opened the door. Grandma had always called her Kancil. Everybody assumed it was because she was small and timid like the *kancil*, the mouse deer that lived in the forest. Grandma told Aryani that she meant the *kancil* in the fables, the clever mouse deer that outwits the bigger, stronger animals by being better with words. "One day you will find your voice, my little Kancil," she would say.

"Come and let me have one last look at you,"

Grandma said, drawing Aryani close. She reached up and brushed Aryani's fringe away from her face. "Why do you wear your hair like that? It hides your lovely eyes. Why don't you wear your hair in a bun like a proper young lady?"

"Oh Grandma, nobody under forty wears their hair like that any more," Aryani said.

"I guess not," Grandma sighed, "but you shouldn't hide your eyes."

"I don't want to go, Grandma." Aryani's voice trembled.

"Oh, come now," said Grandma, patting her hand. "You must be brave, my girl. Your father would be proud of you."

Grandma reached under her pillow and pulled out a small parcel wrapped in a piece of cloth. "I have something for you," she said. "Best keep it a secret, though. Your mother wouldn't understand." She unwrapped the cloth to reveal a necklace.

"Open the window, dear, so you can see it properly," Grandma said.

Aryani took the necklace to the window and pushed the shutters open. The necklace was made from knotted twine. One end of the twine was plaited into a loop, and the other was tied through a tiny cowry shell, which fit snugly through the loop to form the clasp. A polished stone pendant set in a thin frame of tarnished silver hung from the twine. The stone was striped with bands of golden and chocolate brown that shimmered like layers of light. It reminded Aryani of the tiger's eye gem that her uncle wore in a signet ring. Except that her uncle's ring only shone when he held it to the light. The pendant's shimmering light seemed to come from within.

"What is this?" Aryani asked.

The bed creaked as the old woman hauled herself to her feet and joined her granddaughter by the window. Her white hair was pulled into a neat bun, her back was straight and her eyes, though rimmed with the milky blue of old age, were the same colour as her granddaughter's.

"Tiger stone," she whispered. "It has been passed down through our family for many generations."

Grandma clasped her hands around Aryani's, enclosing the pendant. The stone felt strangely warm against Aryani's palm.

"I may never see you again, my little Kancil," said Grandma. Aryani opened her mouth to speak but Grandma silenced her with a shake of her head. "Soon it will be time for me to go. Don't be sad," she said. "I have lived a long life and have had many adventures. It's your turn now. You mustn't wear the necklace until I am gone. When you do, you will understand."

700 YEARS AGO

1

UNDER THE BANYAN TREE

"People call me Kancil after the mouse deer in the fables."

Kancil looked up at Small Aunt, her mother's younger sister. The expression on Small Aunt's face was the same as the one Mother wore when she inspected cloth sold by untrustworthy traders; the traders who chose the badly lit stalls at the back of the market.

"Funny name for a girl," Small Aunt said.

Kancil looked down at her hands. "It was my father's name for me," she said.

"Well, I've never heard of any fables about a *kancil*," Small Aunt sniffed. "What's wrong with your birth name, Sejati? A name that means 'true' is a good name for a girl. Then again, maybe not – people might shorten it to Jati and that means 'teak'. You don't want to draw attention to the colour of your eyes." Small Aunt turned to Mother. "I take it they come from her father – he was that incense seller you were besotted with, wasn't he? Where was he from again?"

For a moment, indignation flashed on Mother's face. Then she bowed her head and made her voice meek. "He was from Sunda, but his father came from over the sea. Kancil and her brother Agus were both blessed with his teak-coloured eyes."

"Hmpf," Small Aunt grunted. "Not much of a blessing."

Kancil had grown up listening to Mother's stories about Small Aunt. About how clever she was. How, by the time she was in her fourteenth year, the same age as Kancil, she already knew what herbs to use to cure almost any illness. Kancil had been looking forward to meeting her and had hoped that they might stay with her, although Mother had said that wasn't possible.

"She left the village to be a servant to a holy woman in the forest many years ago," Mother had said. "We cannot stay with her. We must travel on to Prambanan village and beg shelter from my brother."

Now that she had met Small Aunt, Kancil wasn't so disappointed not to be staying with her. Yet the thought of Prambanan filled her with dread.

She gazed at the path that she and Mother had

followed down the mountainside and out of the forest earlier that morning. She had lost track of how long they had been travelling. It had been many months – first hidden in the clove trader's boat from their home in the Sunda Kingdom to the port of Pekalongan, then in bullock carts and on foot all the way from the coast and over the mountains to reach this place, the Mataram lands, her mother's birthplace, and the most out-of-the-way corner of the Majapahit Kingdom. A place where they would be safe, according to Mother, so long as Kancil could pretend to be someone she wasn't.

"We can trust my sister to keep our secret," Mother had said. "To everyone else you must pretend to be a Majapahit girl. If my brother finds out you have Sunda blood, he won't let us stay and there is nowhere else we can turn."

Kancil had begged to stay in Muara Jati, her home town beside the sea in Sunda. "What will happen when Father and Agus come back? How will they find us?" she had asked.

"They will never return," was all Mother would say.

That seemed like a lifetime ago. Now here they were, sitting under a sprawling banyan tree less than a day's walk from their destination, Prambanan village. It was time for Kancil to show Small Aunt how good she was at pretending to be from Majapahit.

"If my sister is impressed," Mother had said, "then it will be easy to fool my brother." Kancil tried not to think about what would happen if her aunt was unimpressed.

"So tell me your story," Small Aunt commanded in Jawa language.

Everything now depended on Kancil sounding like someone who had been speaking Jawa all her life. Her language lessons had begun in earnest between bouts of seasickness in the hold of the clove trader's boat. Even now, months later, speaking Jawa made her feel a little queasy.

"I was born in the village of Lawucilik, one month's journey east of here," she began shakily. "My father's family were farmers. They took my mother in when she fled Mbah Merapi's wrath many years ago." Kancil took a breath and looked up at the mountain, Mbah Merapi, the volcano that brought both life and death to the Mataram lands. A plume of smoke slipped lazily over the mountain's peak.

"Two months ago the earth swallowed Lawucilik. My father and brother both perished. All I have left is my mother. We return to the village of her birth to beg for shelter."

"And how was it that you and your mother did not perish?"

"We had gone to Trowulan to trade Mother's fine cloth."

"Hmm," said Small Aunt. She turned to Mother, who was leaning against the banyan tree's broad trunk. "The story's not bad. News of what happened to Lawucilik has reached here, so they'll believe you. And it's far enough away that nobody would know you *weren't* there. The part about going to Trowulan is a bit much, though. What if someone asks her what the capital is like?"

"She could make it up," said Mother. "It's not like anyone else from these parts has ever been there."

Small Aunt turned back to Kancil. "Well?" she asked.

Kancil froze. They hadn't practised this part and she had no idea what Trowulan was like. She began to describe her home town, Muara Jati, in Sunda. At least that was a proper town, unlike the ramshackle collections of huts that passed for civilisation in these parts.

"There is a glittering harbour," she said, "full of ships from all over Nusantara and beyond, and in the market you can buy–"

"Enough," Small Aunt said, holding up her hand. "Trowulan is inland, everybody knows that. Why don't you say you went to Bubat? That's somewhere near Trowulan. Nobody here will know it so you can say whatever you like."

Mother turned pale. "Not Bubat," she whispered.

Kancil had been trying to keep her head bowed respectfully. Now she looked up and glared at Small Aunt. How could she be so cruel? Small Aunt looked back at her blankly. Was it possible that she didn't know?

"Why not Bubat?" Small Aunt asked. She looked from Kancil to Mother. "I'm only trying to help."

"It was in Bubat—" Mother began then she fell back against the tree trunk like a spent rice husk. Kancil looked at her anxiously. All the way from Muara Jati Mother had been so strong and determined but now that they had almost reached her village, it was as though the life had drained from her. Her body shook as she tried to suppress a cough.

"It was in Bubat that my father and brother met their fate," Kancil took over from Mother. "They were crew on the ship carrying the King and Queen of Sunda to the marriage of their daughter, Princess Pitaloka, to King Hayam Wuruk of Majapahit. It was a trap. They never returned." The words came out in a rush, as though saying them fast would stop them from hurting. She didn't believe, as Mother did, that both Agus and Father were dead, but thinking about them hurt her just the same.

"I'm sorry, I didn't know. Not much news from the capital makes it this far inland." Small Aunt shrugged.

"It is why we are here," Mother said. "Being from

Majapahit once gave me an advantage in the marketplace in Muara Jati. The other traders thought I must be shrewd because I came from such a sophisticated place." She smiled weakly. "Everything changed after the news came from Bubat. In their grief, our neighbours took revenge on anything they knew to have a Majapahit connection. Our home, my cloth, it was all burned. We were lucky to escape with our lives."

"I see now why you had to leave," said Small Aunt. Then she looked at Kancil with that same look in her eye, as if inspecting poor quality cloth. "Bringing her here was a mistake, though. You've trained her well to speak Jawa, I'll give you that, but she's not good enough – when she's cross she sounds pure Sunda, and you know how people here feel about Sunda. It's for the best that she stays mute. Do you think she can do it? She doesn't seem the type."

"She has done since we reached Pekalongan," Mother replied. "It's not so hard. In our town in Sunda there were three children who could not hear. They had their own language of signs that the other children soon learned. It was like a game. Kancil taught me as we travelled and we manage well enough."

Small Aunt looked doubtful. "It's all very well when it's a game, or when she's travelling and only has to fool people for a day or so before she moves on to the next place. But day-in, day-out? As a fatherless child, it won't be easy for her in the village, you know, and I can't see her holding that tongue of hers for long. Then there are her eyes – it's long enough ago now that people might not make the connection with her father, but even so, there's definitely something a bit *foreign* about them. They will make people wonder where she is from and then it would only take one slip of the tongue for them to realise she's from Sunda."

Kancil had had enough. "What's wrong with being from Sunda?" she fumed. "We had to leave our home because *your* king started a war and made everybody in the Sunda Kingdom hate the Majapahit Kingdom. But what did *we* ever do to *you*?"

Small Aunt shot Mother a look then turned to Kancil. "In *this* land," she said, "children do what they're told and they don't answer back. Perhaps where you come from it's different but you will have to get used to our ways. Whatever happened in Bubat had nothing to do with Prambanan. A feud between the King of Sunda and the King of Majapahit is of no concern to us.

"What *does* concern us is that the only people from Sunda who venture this far east these days are thieves and cheats – bandits, every one. Your father was here when it all began, when the Sunda bandits stole the treasure from the forest temples and brought Mbah Merapi's wrath down on us all. If you hope to find shelter here, the best thing for you to do is keep quiet and pretend you're not from Sunda!"

Kancil looked down at her lap. The indigo dye on her travelling *kain* had faded almost to the colour of the morning sky and it had worn thin and soft, little more than a rag. The cakes of salt and vials of fishpaste that a few sympathetic neighbours had given Mother to trade on their journey were long gone; the basket that Kancil had carried on her back all the way from Muara Jati was empty apart from her good *kain* and *kemben*, her sleeping *sarung* and a shell necklace that she had hidden in the folds of her good clothes when Mother wasn't looking.

Father had made the necklace for her while they sat together on the beach the night before he set sail for the Majapahit Kingdom. He had drilled a hole in each tiny cowry shell with a sharpened fishbone and strung the shells together with sugar palm twine, then he whispered something into each shell before he gave her the necklace. "There," he said. "If you need me while I'm gone, listen to the shells and you will hear my voice." His eyes were twinkling as he said this but they turned sad when Kancil slipped the necklace on. She thought she heard him murmur, "What is lost is lost."

Mother had forbidden Kancil from bringing the

necklace with her. "If they see that in Prambanan, they will guess you're from the Sunda coast," she had said. So Kancil had hidden the necklace and many times during the journey, when she was sure Mother was sleeping, she had carefully unwrapped her treasure and held it close to her ear. Yet she never heard her father's voice.

She sighed. Father was gone and Mother was right; Prambanan was their only hope. So what if Kancil had to keep her mouth shut and her head bowed for the rest of her life? If that was what it took to ensure that they never had to sleep in a ditch again, then she would just have to find a way.

She couldn't let Small Aunt get away with the slight against her home, though; she straightened her back and looked up, fixing her gaze on a point in the distance. "I will do as you say," she said, "and I will prove to you that people from Sunda are *not* all thieves and cheats."

2
CROSSING THE RIVER

From the banyan tree a path led to a river. At first the path was easy to follow; it was well used so the earth was smooth under their bare feet and it led them through a glade of shady ironwood trees. When the path plunged down the steep bank of a ravine their progress slowed. With every step Kancil's basket of provisions thumped against her back and she had to pick her way carefully down the slope, her hands reaching for vines and tree roots to steady herself and stop the basket's weight from sending her tumbling.

She knew she mustn't complain. Her basket was full of gifts from Small Aunt: food for their journey to the village, rare *jamu* ingredients and rich palm sugar to offer Big Uncle's family when they arrived. Mother had tried to say no but Small Aunt insisted. "You'll need them," she said. "You know what they're like." Mother and Small Aunt had shared a knowing look and Kancil wondered anew about Big Uncle, her mother's older brother. On the journey from Sunda, Mother had said little about him. Her silence all the more notable given the praise she lavished on Small Aunt.

The river, when they reached it, was a trickle cutting through the middle of a wide expanse of silt that burned their feet as they trudged across it. They stopped to refill their earthenware *kendi* and cool their feet in the running water before beginning the climb up the other side of the ravine.

The sound of distant thunder was rolling across the treetops when they emerged from the ravine. Mother leaned against a boulder, her eyes squeezed shut. "I'll be fine in a moment," she gasped. She opened her eyes and shook her head. "Come on," she said through gritted teeth. "There's a *pondok* about halfway to the village. If we hurry, we might reach it before the rain." As if on cue, a billowing cloud reached over the mountain to cover the sun, turning the day from bright glare to dull menace.

Fat drops of rain were falling steadily by the time the path led them from the forest to the edge of farmed land. Mother paused to strip two umbrella leaves from a tree. She passed one to Kancil then, holding her own leaf above her head, she set off along a narrow raised path towards the *pondok*: a thatch-roofed shelter on bamboo stilts in the middle of the farmed land. During the planting and harvest seasons, workers would rest here in the midday heat and take shelter from storms like this one. Right now though, the fields were resting and the workers were elsewhere.

The umbrella leaf kept Kancil's head dry and the worst of the rain out of her basket but the rest of her was soaked within minutes. As she hurried along the muddy path, she held out her free hand to catch the raindrops and slurped up quick mouthfuls.

The fields on either side of her were the highest of a series of terraces – shallow basins laid out like huge steps leading down a gentle slope. Between each step water channels had been carefully built and maintained over the years, so the fields could be flooded and drained during the rice-growing season. They were empty now apart from the blackened stalks of a recently harvested dry-season corn crop. Great cracks in the earth soaked up the rain.

Kancil staggered the last few steps to the *pondok*. She slid out of the sling holding the basket to her back and flopped down on the springy split-bamboo floor, letting her muddy feet dangle over the edge. Rain pelted down all around and cascaded off the thatch but the eaves were wide, keeping the open platform dry.

"Here," Mother said, holding out one of Small Aunt's sticky rice parcels. They sat in companionable silence, savouring the best food they had eaten in months.

From the *pondok* the path continued south, down the steps of the terraced rice fields. At the bottom of the hill Kancil could see a bridge across a river and a village gate. She let her eyes slide away from the gate. She didn't want to think about Prambanan yet.

"Do you see the forest temples?" Mother asked, pointing with her chin towards the west. She was doing the same thing as Kancil – avoiding the village. Through the hazy rain, Kancil could make out a dark stone spire reaching up above the forest canopy. The spire was a stepped pyramid. Stone carvings in the shape of elongated bells stood in rows around each level like sentries. At the very top of the spire was a single, massive stone bell. Several smaller spires were just visible through the trees.

Kancil sensed that Mother wanted her to be interested in the temples but her thoughts were elsewhere. She had always been told that her parents met in Mother's village when Father went there to sell frankincense to pilgrims. But the story she had grown up believing – that they had married in the village then gone to the Sunda coast – couldn't be true if Mother planned to make up a story about meeting him in Lawucilik.

Father *must* have been in Mother's village if Small Aunt was worried they might recognise Kancil's "foreign" eyes. Only what was wrong with that? They didn't make her look Sundanese – the teak-brown eyes Kancil shared with Father and her brother, Agus, came from her father's father and where he came from was a mystery. Perhaps in the village they hated anyone who wasn't Majapahit, not just people from Sunda? Or perhaps they had something specifically against Father – but that couldn't be right; everyone loved Father the moment they met him.

Kancil closed her eyes. There are too many questions, she thought. I don't know where to start. Then a strange feeling overcame her; she could hear someone whispering. She looked at Mother to see if she had heard it too but Mother was gazing at the temples. It's only the wind and rain, Kancil told herself. Yet she couldn't help feeling that someone had whispered to her the question she should ask.

She stared at her basket. The necklace! Father! She wanted to cry and at the same time she was furious. All those nights on the journey when she had longed for his voice to comfort her he had stayed silent. Why choose this moment? And why this question? She wanted him to tell her he was alive, that Agus was alive. She wasn't interested in temple treasures. She pursed her lips but

35

now he had put the thought in her mind, she had to ask.

"Mother," she said. "Small Aunt said something about the temple treasures being a reason why Sunda people are hated here. What did she mean?"

Mother nodded. "It happened a long time ago," she said. "There were treasures in the forest temples – ancient gold from when the temples were built. The treasures were kept hidden except for a holy water bowl that was used for special ceremonies. Oh, it was a beautiful thing."

Mother turned to gaze at the temples again.

"And …" Kancil prompted. Her heart was racing. She could feel Father's presence and sense his approval that she had asked the right question. She had to keep Mother talking, if only to keep him near for a little longer.

"The bowl, everything, was stolen. They say the thieves were bandits from Sunda and that has never been forgotten."

"*Were* they from Sunda?" Kancil asked.

Mother shrugged. "Who can say?" she sighed. "Here people think all bandits are from Sunda. In Sunda, people think all pirates are from Samudera. People from Samudera will tell you not to trust anyone from Melayu. It's comforting to think that all bad people are from over the sea, or from the other side of the mountains."

"Was the scoundrel a Sunda bandit?" Kancil asked. She felt giddy. The whispering was so faint that she couldn't be sure she heard anything at all but she felt certain it was her father telling her what to ask.

"What?" Mother's voice was sharp. Kancil flinched.

"It … it was something I heard Small Aunt say to you, something about a scoundrel, the scoundrel. He sounded … bad."

"You shouldn't listen in to other people's conversations," Mother said. She reached for her sleeping *sarung* and wrapped it around her shoulders. "This rain," she grumbled. "It's so cold."

"You used to say it was good that I watched and listened, that it helped you in the market," Kancil murmured.

"I know," Mother's voice was softer now. "That was before. Things are different now. You can watch and listen all you like, but you must be invisible in this village. I'm sorry, child. From now on you must be mute."

Kancil lay down on the *pondok* floor. She could hear a ragged note in her mother's breathing and it made her anxious. She searched her mind for her father's voice to reassure her but there was nobody there. There was never anybody there, she told herself. You imagined hearing him to make yourself feel better.

37

In the stories Father used to tell her, kancil the mouse deer always escaped harm by using words to trick the stronger, more foolish creatures in the forest. I guess in a *real* forest the *real* kancil escapes harm by not being noticed, she thought. She curled her body into a ball. "I can do that," she whispered.

The rain stopped as suddenly as it had begun. Kancil woke to the sound of frogs and insects celebrating the wet season's arrival. She and Mother sat in the *pondok* as though glued in place. Finally, Mother shifted in her seat. "Are you ready?" she asked.

Kancil shook her head.

"Come on," said Mother, "we've got this far without being attacked by bandits or tigers. The spirits must be on our side."

Kancil stretched her tired body. Father had once told her, "My father came from a land of tigers, far, far away. When he was shipwrecked on the wild coast of Sunda he heard a tiger growl and he knew he had come to a good place. The tiger is a noble creature. It can see into your soul. If your heart is pure and your intentions are good, you have nothing to fear."

Mother had snorted when she heard him say this. "The tiger," she said, "is a wild beast. If you see one, you should climb the nearest tree."

Kancil had never seen a tiger herself but she liked to believe that her father's tigers had been keeping them safe from bandits on their journey through the forest. Somehow she felt they would be more loyal than the spirits.

Mother was rustling about in the baskets. "You should wear your good *kain* to enter the village," she said. "We want to make a good impression."

Suddenly, Kancil was on her feet, lunging towards her basket. Too late. As Mother pulled out the *kain* she flicked it to shake out the folds. Kancil's shell necklace tumbled through the air, bounced twice on the floor then slipped through a gap between the bamboo slats. Kancil lay flat on the floor and peered between the slats just in time to see the string of tiny cowry shells disappear, sucked by its own weight under the surface of the silty, rain-softened earth.

"What was that?" Mother demanded. The tone of her voice suggested that she knew exactly what it was.

"My necklace," sobbed Kancil. She didn't care if she wasn't meant to speak. "The one Father gave me before he left for Bubat." She cried out in pain as Mother dragged her up by the arm and spun her around.

"You foolish girl!" Mother fumed. "*Sea*shells! You're supposed to be from Lawucilik. From the mountains. The *Majapahit* mountains!" She shook her daughter so hard that Kancil's teeth rattled. "If my brother found this necklace, he would know I lied to him about where you are from. That alone would be enough for him to throw us out. And what do you think would happen if he figured out you're not only from the coast, you're from the *Sunda* coast?"

Kancil didn't know what would happen and she could tell from the look on Mother's face that she didn't want to find out.

With one last shake, Mother let go of Kancil's shoulders, sending her tumbling back onto the bamboo floor. Mother climbed down the steps to the ground below and began to squeeze through the posts that held the *pondok* up above the muddy earth.

"What are you doing?" Kancil gasped.

"I'm going to find that necklace and I'm going to smash it to pieces. We can't risk anyone finding it," Mother replied.

"No! Please!" Kancil begged. She was thinking fast. "It's … it's a sign from the spirits. My necklace is like Lawucilik; it has been swallowed by the earth. It's the spirits' way of saying they'll go along with our story. Please don't smash it! If anyone finds it, they won't know it's mine. Please, please let it stay buried in the mud." She knew she was babbling but she couldn't stop. It was bad enough to lose her father's last gift to a muddy field.

If the necklace was smashed, her heart would break.

Mother sighed and squeezed back out from under the *pondok*. "Look at us," she said, shaking her head. "If that's all it takes to make you speak, what hope is there?"

Kancil sat up and faced her mother. She made two fists and banged them together: the sign for "no". Then she mimed her mother shaking her and touched one hand to her chest to sign "me". She touched her chest again, banged her fists then opened and closed the fingers of one hand, like a bird's beak.

"Don't shake me and I won't speak?" asked Mother.

Kancil nodded.

"Don't *provoke* me and I'll have no cause to shake you!" Mother said, but the anger had gone from her voice. "Pass me my *kain*," she continued. "I'll have to change down here. My feet are all muddy, thanks to you."

Kancil passed her the betel and indigo dyed cloth and picked up her own *kain* from the floor. She took a deep breath before she wrapped the *kemben* around her chest.

This is the last free breath I will ever take, she thought.

3

THROUGH THE GATE

Kancil followed her mother over the bridge and between the arching bamboo poles that formed the village gate. Just inside the gate was a rickety structure that might once have been a village meeting place. It was shaped like a *pendopo* with a peaked roof held up by sturdy pillars above an open platform. The tops of the pillars and the roof beams were ornately carved but there were holes in the thatch and puddles from the recent rain had formed on the earthen floor.

"When I was a girl …" Mother began, then her voice trailed off and she turned away from the *pendopo*. "Best not to look back," she said as she headed into the village.

A steady stream of villagers was walking in the same direction. Some looked their way with mild interest but only briefly; clearly there was something more exciting going on than the appearance of two weary travellers. Kancil turned to Mother for an explanation. Mother shrugged.

Kancil looked around as they walked along the tree-lined path. The village was bigger than she had expected; they had already passed six or eight houses on the main path and smoke was rising from the kitchen fires in many more homes along smaller paths hidden among the trees.

Further along, a crowd had gathered around a *pendopo* that stood in front of the high fence of a grand house. The *pendopo* was smaller than the one at the village gate yet even from a distance, Kancil could see that it was better kept.

Mother reached down and gripped Kancil's hand. "That's your uncle's house," she breathed.

"What's the news?" Mother asked a grey-haired woman at the back of the crowd when they reached the *pendopo*.

"A messenger has come from the king's palace," said the woman without turning around.

Kancil tried to see through gaps in the crowd. It was a solid wall of bodies, all standing on tiptoes to see over the people in front. The lucky ones with a view relayed the scene unfolding in the *pendopo* to those behind them.

"He's carrying the Majapahit seal."

"He's reading from a *lontar* scroll."

"What's he saying, Ki Sardu?" someone asked, directing the question at a man who was wearing the white headdress of a priest.

The priest stroked his wispy beard, his brow creased in concentration. The messenger was using the polite Jawa language. All Majapahit officials were expected to know the polite language but few villagers understood beyond the standard phrases recited at ceremonies.

"He has a message from a prince," the priest said solemnly. Kancil rolled her eyes. *She* could have told them that. "The Prince of Mataram," the priest continued, "... the n*ew* Prince of Mataram – Bhre Mataram – is coming to claim his title!"

The crowd gasped in unison.

"Where is Mataram?" a boy asked his father.

"*Tsk*! *This* is Mataram," the father replied, waving his arm around to take in the village, the rice fields and the mountain beyond.

"Is it my brother who he is speaking to?" Mother said quietly to the grey-haired woman.

The woman turned around sharply and her mouth dropped open. "Is it really you, Su?" she gasped.

"Yes, Ibu Tari," said Mother. "It's me."

The older woman reached out to touch Mother's

arm, as if to convince herself she was real. "Oh, my dear, we thought you had perished."

Mother bowed her head, "I'm sorry, Ibu, I didn't mean to— I was separated from my family when Mbah Merapi unleashed his fury. And then … and then I wanted to get as far away as possible. In Lawucilik, we heard no news and I feared what I might find if I came back."

"You were in Lawucilik?" Ibu Tari's eyes were wide. "Well," she said after a pause, "you must be blessed to survive disaster twice."

Kancil sensed Mother's discomfort. Lying to people she knew was different to making up stories for strangers on the journey from Sunda.

"This is my daughter," Mother said to change the subject. Kancil kept her head bowed as she had been taught. She could feel Ibu Tari looking at her and for a moment she was tempted to raise her eyes and speak just to see what the reaction would be. She felt her mother's grip tightening on her hand. "My daughter doesn't speak," said Mother.

There was an awkward silence. "Your husband?" Ibu Tari asked softly.

"Lost when the earth swallowed Lawucilik," Mother replied. "Together with my son."

"Oh," said the older woman. Kancil could tell from

Ibu Tari's voice that she no longer thought they were blessed.

The crowd had grown, with at least one hundred people jostling for a view of the *pendopo*. As those behind pushed forwards, Kancil struggled to stay upright. For a moment a gap in the crowd opened. She dropped Mother's hand and began to squeeze through to the front to see what was going on. The gap closed and Kancil only succeeded in wedging herself into a dark forest of arms and legs with somebody's elbow poking into her neck. The suffocating smell of hard-working bodies engulfed her.

Unable to turn around, she backed out of the crowd. Someone stepped on the edge of her *kain*, pulling it loose. She crouched awkwardly and tried to rewrap it, but the crowd surged towards the *pendopo* and she was caught off balance. Suddenly, she found herself sprawled on the ground, clutching at her unravelling *kain*.

A huge pair of hands plucked her from the dirt. "Is this your daughter, Su?" she heard a booming voice above her say. "Or is it a chicken having a dirt bath?" The voice belonged to a hairy giant. He was the closest thing to an ogre that Kancil had ever seen, and she had to press her lips shut to suppress a scream.

Laughter bubbled through the crowd and a boy poked Kancil in the chest. "Chicken," he screeched, flapping his arms like a demented bird and hopping from one foot to the other. Kancil wanted to shove him into the dirt, but one hand was holding her *kain* together and the other was gripping the giant's leg for balance. All she could do was glare at the boy. As their eyes met, he hesitated, a strange look on his face – it wasn't the usual curious stare she got when people noticed her eyes for the first time, it was something more like recognition. Kancil held her breath, waiting for him to say something about her eyes but he barely missed a beat before crowing, "Oooh, scary chicken."

"Shut up, boy," a woman said, swatting him over the head.

Mother's hands were at Kancil's waist, expertly rearranging her *kain*. "Be careful!" she whispered. "Please! Stay close, and *don't* draw attention to yourself!"

Kancil's cheeks burned with embarrassment and fury and she swallowed hard to stop from bursting into tears. Do I have to *cry* silently too? she wondered.

Suddenly, the giant scooped her up onto his shoulder. Kancil yelped with surprise. "Hey–!" She managed to swallow her words before she said "put me down". Even so, everybody was staring at her. Kancil knew she was small for her age, but did the giant really think she was young enough to be bounced around like this?

"I thought you said she doesn't speak," said the giant.

Kancil looked down at her mother, who was looking back at her in horror. "She ... she doesn't," Mother replied after a moment. "Not words, just ... sounds."

"Oh," said the giant, nodding. "That's too bad. For a moment I thought I had cured her." The people nearby seemed to have forgotten about the *pendopo* now that they had a new spectacle to entertain them.

"What's wrong with her eyes?" a child asked.

"Shhh!" an adult voice replied. "She's been cursed."

Kancil was taken aback. She could understand the muteness being explained as a curse, but her eyes were another matter. They were her father's eyes; they were no curse!

The crowd was losing interest now. Only the boy who had teased her was still looking at her, a thoughtful expression on his face. Kancil made a point of ignoring him, raising her chin and looking down over the crowd into the *pendopo*. Being treated like a child wasn't so bad if it meant she got the best view.

The messenger, wearing the *sarung* and headdress of a Majapahit official, was standing on the first step of the *pendopo*. He was reading a message that had been carved into strips of *lontar* leaf. Each strip was sewn to the next with fine palm thread so that when folded, the leaves formed a neat stack. The messenger gradually unfolded leaf after leaf as his voice droned on. Polite Jawa language was a lot like polite Sunda language, Kancil decided. It took ten times longer to say anything than if you were speaking the everyday language. The priest had stopped translating. Perhaps the language became too difficult for him or perhaps he had grown bored with it. Nobody in the crowd seemed to be paying much attention. They were chattering about what the arrival of a prince would mean for the village.

"It's just what we need to bring some order to the place," said one.

"Absolutely," agreed another, "it's only a matter of time before those forest bandits run out of travellers to rob and turn their attention to us."

"Did he say what happened to the old Bhre?" someone asked. "Don't you think it was a bit strange that he stopped visiting all those years ago and never sent word?"

"The messenger said he died," the priest weighed in. "He was quite old the last time he was here, if you remember. And they've had other things to contend with in the capital – those Sunda pirates have been causing trouble again."

There was a general muttering about evil Sunda in the crowd. Kancil shrank back against the giant's shoulder.

"He never used to stay long, did he, the old Bhre?" It was the giant who spoke this time. "Just long enough to make sure he was getting his fair share of the harvest and to eat us out of livestock. Then he'd be off." His comment drew a ripple of laughter and Kancil had to hold on tight as the giant jiggled with mirth.

"*Ssshh*!" scolded the priest. "Don't be coarse. The messenger will think we're peasants."

"Oh, we wouldn't want him to think that, would we?" the giant chuckled.

The chatter continued and the messenger droned on so Kancil turned her attention instead to the man seated in the centre of the *pendopo*. He too was wearing the garb of a Majapahit official, although Kancil could see that his *sarung* was a little moth-eaten. Nevertheless, he sat proudly on his ornately carved stool, his fists resting on his knees, shoulders back and chin jutting forwards. So that's Big Uncle, she thought. He looked very important.

Finally, the messenger stopped talking and folded the *lontar* scroll. There was an expectant hush. Big Uncle cleared his throat and began to speak. Kancil could tell he wasn't comfortable speaking the polite Jawa language; he shifted in his seat and cleared his throat every few words. From her position on the north side of the *pendopo* she could see one side of the messenger's face. She thought his lip curled into a sneering smile but she couldn't be sure.

"What did Bapak Thani say?" someone called out.

"Oh, er, he just invited the messenger in to refresh himself for the journey back to the capital," the priest replied.

Kancil watched as the messenger followed Big Uncle through the *pendopo* and down into the fenced courtyard in front of the house. A women and a girl who had been kneeling behind Big Uncle's seat stood up and followed them. They were both well dressed and their necks and wrists were laden with jewellery. The woman looked to be a little older than Mother but the girl was young, perhaps a year or two older than Kancil.

"Did you see your aunt and your cousin?" asked Mother when the giant deposited Kancil back on the ground. Kancil nodded and looked at her feet – her dirty, travel-worn, mud-caked feet. From the brief glimpse of her relatives, she could tell it would take more than silence to hide the fact that she didn't belong here. Kancil had expected to feel superior to her mother's family, living as they did in such a remote place. Yet her aunt and her cousin were both so elegant. Their skin was the colour of ripe sawo fruit; the colour of ladies who sat in pavilions all day and had servants to attend to life's mundane tasks, not the colour of travellers who had walked for months under a scorching dry-season sun.

Kancil closed her eyes and willed herself back to

Sunda, playing in the shallows at sundown and climbing coconut trees with Agus when Mother wasn't around to remind her to be a lady. When she opened her eyes all she saw was a glowering mountain and towering trees. She was trapped.

The crowd had dispersed now that the spectacle was over and night was drawing in, but the giant and the grey-haired lady were still there. "You know you can stay with us," said the giant. "We'll find room."

"Thank you, Bapak Pohon," said Mother, bowing respectfully. "You are very kind, but we should stay with our family."

Ibu Tari, the grey-haired lady, nodded in agreement. "It is the proper thing to do," she said.

4

BIG UNCLE'S HOUSE

"Follow my lead," Mother said to Kancil when Bapak Pohon and Ibu Tari had left. She smoothed her *kain* and walked up the steps to the *pendopo* with her head held high. She untied her basket and took Kancil's from her back. Then she removed the parcels of *jamu* and palm sugar and laid them on the floor in front of the solid timber bench where Big Uncle had sat.

"Greetings, my brother," she called in a clear voice as she kneeled facing the closed gate and bowed her head.

Kancil kneeled beside her. With her head tucked in and her nose touching her knees she couldn't see a thing. She could hear snatches of voices coming from beyond the fence but the *pendopo* was silent.

Mother cleared her throat. "Greetings, my brother," she called again, more loudly this time. The sounds from inside stopped. Someone barked a command. Kancil heard footsteps accompanied by the tap of a walking cane and the rattle of the gate being unlatched.

She twisted her neck so she could see while keeping her forehead pressed to the ground. In the gloomy evening light all she could make out was a stooped woman standing in the shadows behind the gate.

"What?" snapped the woman.

"I am Sumirah, younger sister of Bapak Thani. My home is destroyed and all I have in the world is my mute daughter. I throw myself on the mercy of my good brother."

"Wait here," the woman said. The gate swung shut behind her and Kancil listened to her retreating footsteps, then to the silence that stretched on and on.

By the time the gate creaked open again it was almost dark and Kancil's legs had gone to sleep. She heard heavy footsteps then a grunt as someone sat down on the bench.

"What do you want?" Kancil recognised the voice as Big Uncle's, although he was speaking the ordinary Jawa language now.

"We throw ourselves on your mercy, Brother," said Mother. Her voice was muffled as she kept her head low to the floor.

"Speak up, I can't hear you," Big Uncle grumbled.

Mother raised her head slightly and took a deep breath. When she spoke, she spoke evenly. It reminded Kancil of times when her own brother, Agus, had teased her or got her into trouble, and she had been forced to show respect to him because he was older, even though all she wanted to do was punch him.

"My husband and son are dead, swallowed by the earth in Lawucilik. I have come home with my daughter to beg you for shelter. We will work hard. You will not regret being compassionate." She smothered a cough.

"Hmpf," Big Uncle snorted. "Where were you when your mother was dying?"

"Forgive me, Brother."

"And your father."

"Forgive me, Brother."

"All very well for you to run off to who knows where when things got tough. Some of us had to stay behind and rebuild this place after that scoundrel … well, *some* of us were loyal."

"Forgive me, Brother. I did not mean to abandon my family. I became lost in the confusion when we all ran from Mbah Merapi's anger. I could not find my way to the usual refuge. I know it has been many years but I am here now and wish to repay my debt to my family. My daughter will be no trouble; she will work hard. We will both work hard."

"Who was her father?"

Kancil felt a foot prod her outstretched hands and she flinched.

"He–" Mother's voice broke, "he was a farmer in Lawucilik. He was a good man."

"Is she simple?"

"Pardon?"

"Is she simple? I was told she is dumb. Is she half-witted?"

Why hadn't Mother accepted the giant's offer to stay with him? Kancil wondered.

"She hasn't spoken since the earth took her father and brother but she is not simple." Kancil was relieved to hear the indignation in her mother's voice. "She can cook and clean and she learns fast. I can teach her to weave. We can be of service to Big Sister, lighten her load in preparation for the prince's arrival."

"Wait here," sighed Big Uncle as he heaved himself from the bench, picked up the gifts and stomped out of the *pendopo*.

Kancil rolled over onto her hip. Pins and needles shot through her legs. She winced but stopped herself from crying out. Mother was curled in a ball, her face pressed into her knees as she coughed uncontrollably. Kancil reached out to touch her shoulder and eventually the coughing subsided.

"It's just the damp air," Mother whispered. "I'll be fine."

Just as Kancil was beginning to think they would be spending the night in the *pendopo*, a young servant appeared. "This way," she said, holding the gate open with one hand. In her other hand she held a candlenut lamp, but as soon as they entered the courtyard she turned around to light her own path. Kancil and Mother stumbled behind her down a dark passageway leading between the main house and a row of small shacks.

The servant stopped at the last shack. It had a thatched roof held up by four thick bamboo poles. Palm mats hanging from the roof formed makeshift walls on three sides. A bamboo platform, barely big enough for Kancil and Mother to lie on side by side, was lashed to two of the poles and held up above the packed earth floor by rough-sawn logs. "You sleep here," said the servant. She turned back towards the house, leaving them in the dark.

Kancil flopped down on the sleeping platform. The whole structure shook, disturbing the chickens that were roosting in the next shack. The chickens' squawking and flapping set off the pigs in a sty nearby. Kancil groaned.

"It could be worse," Mother murmured.

Kancil raised herself onto her elbows and peered

at her mother in the faint moonlight. "How?" she mouthed.

"Well …" said Mother, "we could be sleeping *in* the pigsty."

It felt like only moments later that Mother was gently shaking Kancil awake. A rooster was crowing and the early morning air was fresh and clean. Kancil rubbed her eyes and sat up.

"Stay here, I'll be back soon," Mother said.

Kancil peeked through the gaps between the palm mat walls and the bamboo corner posts. To the east was the shack where the chickens roosted and beyond that the passageway she had walked down the night before. A grove of mango and papaya trees flanked the north and west sides of the sleeping shack. Through the trees she could make out the shape of the pigsty and the fence that formed the rear boundary of the property.

The south side of her new home faced into the yard, where chickens pecked at the ground and squabbled under a shady tamarind tree. Mother walked around the tamarind tree and into a hut at the back of the main house. Kancil guessed it must be the kitchen.

Suddenly, the chickens started squawking and flapping in alarm and moments later a gate in the back fence swung open. The servant who had shown them to their shack the previous night entered the yard with a load of firewood tied to her back. Kancil guessed she was only about four years older than herself, though her scowling expression made her look much older. The girl passed Kancil, close enough to call out a polite greeting, but she looked straight at her without even a nod. Kancil stared at her retreating back, not quite believing the look of disdain she had seen on the girl's face. She was a *servant* and she dared treat Kancil like that when her uncle was the head of the household? The reality of her situation was beginning to dawn on Kancil – she might be a relation but she was a poor relation: poor, fatherless and mute.

5

THE KITCHEN

After a breakfast of dry rice scrapings from yesterday's pot, Kancil and Mother followed a path that led from the back gate, through a tangle of bamboo and vines, then down a steep embankment to the river. The sound of women and children splashing and chattering grew louder as they approached. They emerged from the undergrowth at a point where a wide bend in the river formed a bathing pool.

There was a momentary lull in the women's conversations when the newcomers stepped into the pool, but Ibu Tari, the grey-haired lady, was there and she greeted them warmly. Taking their cue from Ibu Tari, the women nodded and smiled at Mother while the children stared at Kancil. She tried to ignore them as she scrubbed her feet with a pumice stone.

The bathers' attention shifted to a woman who was coming down the path. She walked with a cane, which she jabbed at the ground with every step as though to remind the earth of its faults. "That's Bibi," Mother whispered. "Be careful of her."

As Bibi reached the pool she gave Mother a curt nod. "The loom is ready in the front pavilion. Ibu Thani will be waiting for you," she said. At the sound of her voice, Kancil recognised her as the woman who had first come to the gate the previous night. Now Bibi turned her attention to Kancil. "And *she* can wait for me in the kitchen." Then she stepped onto the path that led upstream to the washing pool, saying loudly enough for everybody to hear, "Though what I'm supposed to do with bandit spawn is beyond me."

Kancil looked to Mother for an explanation, but Mother avoided her gaze. Her mouth was set in a thin line and she was blinking back tears.

The kitchen was a low-roofed hut. Inside it was dark and hot. The air reeked with the smells of fishpaste and hot coconut oil and the combination made Kancil's stomach turn. The skinny boy who had humiliated her at the *pendopo* was sitting on the floor inside the doorway. When he saw Kancil he grinned. She glared back at him.

She could hear Bibi huffing up the path so she waited by the doorway, trying not to look at the boy though she could feel his eyes on her. Bibi didn't greet either of them when she arrived, she just walked into the kitchen, grumbling under her breath. After a moment's hesitation, Kancil followed her.

At the back of the hut a wall panel hinged open to allow some sunlight into the gloom, and beneath this makeshift window was a stone fireplace. The girl servant Kancil had seen that morning sat on a stool before the fire. Her elbows rested on her knees and in one hand she held a ladle, dangling it in a pan full of boiling liquid. She made sporadic efforts to stir the liquid but her eyelids fluttered and her head drooped in the heat.

Bibi slapped the girl over the head and screeched, "Ida! You moron, it's burning!" The startled girl sat up and began stirring frantically. "No, you idiot, it's too late for that." Bibi grabbed the ladle with her free hand. "Go get the washing in before it rains." Ida stood and stumbled towards the door. With a grunt, Bibi hoisted the heavy pan off the grate and tipped the blackened contents down the drain that led under the wall of the hut.

The boy in the doorway was chuckling to himself. Ida snarled at him as she passed.

"Why so cross?" the boy asked. "You got what you wanted, a nice walk in the fresh air." He ducked as she reached out to hit him then went back to his work shelling nuts. Yesterday he had worn a *sarung* over his left shoulder. Now he was bare-chested and when he leaned into the light, Kancil could see that his shoulder was twisted and that he lifted his left arm awkwardly. Three parallel scars marked the left side of his chest.

"Don't stand there gaping," Bibi huffed at Kancil. "Take this." She thrust the ladle into Kancil's hand and pushed her onto the stool. Kancil gazed at the iron pan as Bibi poured strained coconut milk into it from a gourd.

"Oh, for goodness sake, don't tell me you don't know how to make coconut oil!" Bibi took the ladle and shoved Kancil out of the way, sending her tumbling from the stool. Kancil managed to regain her balance before she fell into the fire. She shuffled to a spot on the dirt floor, close enough to see the pan but far enough away to be out of Bibi's reach.

"Don't let it burn like that idiot Ida did. You have to keep stirring it *all* the time." Bibi spoke loudly, pronouncing each word slowly while she gave an exaggerated demonstration of stirring the pot. Kancil wished she could tell her that she wasn't deaf or stupid.

Bibi skimmed a spoonful of coconut grease from the surface of the cooking liquid and dropped it into a bowl. "And these," she said, scooping out two golden nuggets of coconut candy that had formed in the bubbling liquid, "don't let *him* get them." She bent her head towards the boy in the doorway as she scraped the nuggets onto a banana leaf. "He's worse than a nest of ants."

Kancil flinched as Bibi lunged towards her, grabbed her by the shoulder and steered her back onto the stool. Bibi stood behind her for a while, watching her stir and skim the oil. Then she stomped away, taking a swipe at the boy in the doorway as she went. He ducked instinctively.

"Why didn't you keep Ida awake? She could have burned down the kitchen," Bibi snapped.

"Oh, don't worry, Bibi," the boy replied. "My tiger spirit had everything under control." He clawed the air with his hands and laughed loudly at his own joke.

"Imbecile," Bibi muttered as she left.

"Not bad for a beginner."

Kancil jumped and the ladle clattered against the pan. She hadn't heard the boy creep up behind her. She had not forgotten how he had humiliated her outside the *pendopo* and didn't want him to feel he had the advantage now. She turned away, raising her chin dismissively.

The boy stayed close – just on the edge of her vision.

It was impossible to ignore him. Kancil changed her tactics and shifted on the stool so she could stare back at him while watching the pan out of the corner of her eye. She guessed that he was about the same age as her, although it was difficult to tell. His impish grin made him appear younger while his wiry frame and tanned face belonged to someone who had already spent many years doing hard physical work.

Kancil inspected his left arm closely; it was thinner than his right arm and the shoulder was crooked. She turned her attention to the parallel scars on his chest and then to a much more recent wound on his ribs.

The boy followed her gaze. "Oh, that, do you like it?" he said, raising his arm so she could see the wound properly. "That one came courtesy of Bibi on a bad day." He turned so the light fell on the marks on his chest. "My tiger stripes are prettier though, don't you think?" Unlike the jagged scar on his ribs, the raised scars on his chest were smooth and even, as though they had been carved with a very sharp knife. Or very sharp claws.

"As I was saying," the boy continued, standing up and peering into the pan, "you're doing a very good job so don't pay any attention when Bibi comes in and calls you an idiot."

Kancil's eyes kept straying to the boy's scars. "I know you don't speak," the boy continued, "so I'll just answer the questions that you want to ask. You're not deaf, are you?"

Kancil shook her head.

"Best keep your eye on that," he said, nodding towards the pan, "or you'll cop it from Bibi." Kancil turned back to stirring the oil just in time.

"They call me Kitchen Boy because nobody knows my name. Not that having a name means anyone round here will use it. You've probably figured that out by now. Anyway, nobody knows my name because your Small Aunt, the crazy one so they say, found me in the forest when I was a baby. She disturbed a tigress and cub when she was out looking for herbs and she thought she was done for. Then the tigress stood up and walked away. It turned out the cub was me.

"Your aunt couldn't take me home with her so she brought me here and convinced your other aunt – the snooty one – that I was charmed and my presence here would protect the household from marauding tigers. They were sending me out to the forest to collect pepper and honey pretty much as soon as I could walk – apparently their last pepper collector got eaten."

Kitchen Boy told his story like he thought it was a good joke, but then he seemed to think everything was a joke. Maybe he'd figured out that was the best way to cope with Bibi. Kancil wondered whether he kept up the act when he was in the forest. Going out there alone must be even more frightening than facing up to Bibi every day, especially with only one fully functioning arm.

Kancil felt the frustration of not being allowed to speak more keenly now than she had since she arrived in Prambanan. There were so many questions she wanted to ask. Had his arm always been like that? Had a tiger's claws really caused the scars on his chest? And did nobody know who his parents were? She would have liked to tell him that tigers were special for her too. That her father's father had been a tiger charmer. On second thought, she probably wouldn't tell him that. He would laugh at her, she could tell from the teasing way he spoke.

She glanced at him to get a better look at his twisted shoulder, just in time to see his good hand steal the last of the coconut nuggets that she had been carefully piling on the banana leaf. Kancil gasped at the empty plate and slapped at his retreating hand with the ladle.

Kitchen Boy yelped and leaped back, sucking the back of his hand where the hot oil had burned him. "*Pah*!" he spat. "I was wrong about you. You're like all the rest." He retreated to his stool and took a small medicine box from a hiding place in the wall. Muttering to himself, he dabbed ointment on his hand.

Kancil was sorry to have hurt him but she was

relieved that she hadn't forgotten herself and shouted. She scraped at the bottom of the pan to coax more nuggets into life. It was no use, they would only appear when they were ready. Kancil gulped back tears. Don't be stupid, she told herself. Bibi's only a servant. How badly can she beat me?

By the time the thump of Bibi's cane on the path announced her return, Kancil had extracted nearly all the coconut oil and a small pile of nuggets rested on the banana leaf. Bibi stomped to the stove to inspect Kancil's work.

"Where are the rest?" she demanded as she peered at the banana leaf. She scooped up the nuggets and popped them into her mouth. As she turned to go, she gave Kancil's ear a stinging slap.

Ida entered the kitchen. She spooned rice from the steamer onto two banana leaves, sprinkled some dried fish onto the dishes then followed Bibi outside to sit on the bamboo day bed under the eaves.

Wondering whether she should follow suit, Kancil looked to Kitchen Boy for her cue. He stood up and brushed down his *sarung*, then he walked with exaggerated dignity to the rice steamer. His movements were a perfect imitation of the way Kancil's aunt and cousin had left the *pendopo* yesterday. Kancil was smiling at his performance when his expression changed to one of mock fury and he tapped the rice spoon sharply against the steamer. He wasn't mocking her cousin; he was mocking her.

Kancil felt tears prickling behind her eyes. How *dare* he! Kitchen Boy strode back to his place near the door with his head up and chest puffed out like a hero. Or like some stupid rooster, thought Kancil. She fetched herself some rice and went to join the others. As she passed Kitchen Boy she gave him her deadliest glare. He laughed so hard he nearly choked on a mouthful of rice.

Bibi and Ida turned around to see what was causing the commotion. "What's wrong with you, moron?" said Ida, tossing a galangal root at Kitchen Boy's head. He snapped at it with his teeth but missed; the galangal bounced off his cheek and rolled away.

Looking around for somewhere to sit, Kancil settled on a large log that was positioned close to the kitchen wall. It was low enough for her to show respect to Bibi and Ida but gave her a height advantage over Kitchen Boy.

An onion hit her on the head almost as soon as she sat down. "You have no idea, do you, Bandit Spawn?" said Bibi. "Get down off that." Defeated, Kancil slipped down from the log, squatting on her heels to keep her *kain* out of the dirt. She stared hungrily at her rice but there was a lump in her throat that no food could get past.

Kitchen Boy sidled closer to her and she braced herself for more taunting. She watched his hand reach into the waist-fold of his *sarung*, remove a banana-leaf package and place it on her plate. His movement was so subtle and fluid that Kancil wouldn't have noticed if she hadn't been watching closely.

Half-expecting a spider to leap from it, Kancil carefully unfolded the leaf. Inside were four golden-brown coconut nuggets. She stared at them for a moment, trying to make sense of this strange boy. She stole a glance at Bibi and Ida to make sure they weren't watching. Then, trying her best to be as subtle as Kitchen Boy, she took two of the nuggets and placed them on his plate.

6

PAYING RESPECT

Kancil survived her first day in the kitchen with only a few burns on her arms from spitting coconut oil. She endured insults from Bibi and teasing from Kitchen Boy without uttering a word – although her teeth had shredded the inside of her cheeks with the effort of staying silent and her head ached from the tears she was determined not to shed. Finally, Bibi released her for the day and she made her way back to the tiny shack, hoping that she might be allowed to lie on the floor undisturbed for the rest of her life.

Her hopes were dashed. Mother was already there, dressed in her good *kain*. "We must pay our respects to your aunt and your cousin, Citra," said Mother. Kancil groaned and her shoulders slumped.

Mother began to comb Kancil's hair but she had to

stop when a spasm of coughing racked her body. "It's the evening air," she said in response to Kancil's look of concern. "I'll be fine in the morning."

The front courtyard looked beautiful in the early evening light and the scent of night blossoms hung in the air. Big Aunt and Citra were lounging in the pavilion nestled among hibiscus trees, where Mother had spent the day weaving. They were sipping *jamu* from polished clay cups and Bibi was kneading Big Aunt's shoulders while Ida crouched on the step, massaging Citra's feet.

Kancil's body ached from her day in the kitchen. She would love to be in her aunt's or cousin's place, yet neither of them looked happy. Big Aunt was giving Citra a lesson in the polite Jawa language. "No! That's *wrong*," she said. "You have to speak slowly and softly, and don't open your mouth so wide …"

"It's too difficult," Citra whined. "And you're hurting my foot!" She kicked Ida's hand away and reached for a sliver of palm sugar to take away the bitterness of the *jamu* health tonic she was drinking.

Citra glared at Kancil. "What are *you* staring at?" she demanded. Kancil bowed her head and crouched a little lower.

"Greetings, my sister," said Mother, kneeling at the step of the pavilion and touching her forehead to the floor.

It's all just an act, Kancil reminded herself; Mother doesn't think any better of them than I do.

At that moment Big Uncle emerged from the house and strode over to the pavilion. He looked more relaxed in his plain *sarung* than he had in his official's outfit the day before, but he still had the air of someone accustomed to being obeyed. He had oiled his balding head as well as his moustache and he seemed to shine in the evening light. "How is the lesson going?" he asked.

"Why do I have to learn this stupid language, anyway? It's too hard," Citra blurted. Kancil heard an irritated "*tsk*" under her aunt's breath.

Big Uncle spoke gently to the girl. "Now, now, child. I know it's difficult, but it will be worth it in the end. You must be able to speak polite Jawa if you are to marry a prince."

Kancil choked back a laugh. He couldn't seriously believe that a prince would marry a village girl, even one as stuck-up as Citra.

"Why don't you let my sister take over the tuition, my dear?" Big Uncle was talking to his wife now. "You look tired, and she might as well make herself useful."

Mother climbed into the pavilion. Bibi and Ida were looking down at Kancil, their eyes glittering. Kancil guessed they were hoping she would try to follow Mother so they could crow over her ignorance

– but she knew her place. She sat back on her heels with her hands folded in her lap and her head bowed. Disappointing Bibi and Ida was a small victory, but a victory nonetheless.

"You there, girl!" It took Kancil a moment to realise that Big Uncle was talking to her. "Tamarind water," he ordered. Then he stepped through the gate to the *pendopo* that was already buzzing with men's voices.

As evening turned to night, Kancil was kept busy running back and forth from kitchen to *pendopo* with drinks and snacks. Every man in the village had come to Big Uncle's *pendopo* to receive their orders from the village elders in preparation for the prince's arrival.

Big Uncle and three other village elders sat on a mat in the middle of the *pendopo*. On Big Uncle's right sat Ki Sardu, the priest who had translated for the crowd the previous day. His calendar was laid out in front of him and as each task was discussed, he gazed thoughtfully at the symbols carved into the *lontar* leaves before announcing a suitable date for the task to commence.

On Big Uncle's left sat a man whose role, as far as Kancil could figure out, was to agree with everything Big Uncle said. "*Iya, Iyaaaa*," he murmured approvingly, bobbing his head up and down whenever Big Uncle spoke. Kancil decided to call him Bapak Iya.

The fourth elder sat a little apart from the others. He had a wispy white beard and wore a holy man's headdress. Kancil thought he might be the oldest person she had ever seen. He said very little and at first Kancil wondered if he was asleep. Yet, before any important decision was reached, the other elders would turn to him. If he inclined his head slightly, the other men would nod approvingly and the matter would be settled. If he tilted his head to one side and looked up to the rafters with a puzzled expression on his face, the men would sigh and continue their discussion.

It was only when Bibi ordered her to take a cup of ginger tea to the *juru kunci* that Kancil figured out who he was. Mother had told her about the *juru kunci*, the seer who communicated with the spirits to interpret the moods of the mountain, Mbah Merapi, and advise the villagers how to respond.

Gradually the crowd dispersed, leaving the elders alone in the *pendopo*.

"This is an important opportunity for us," Big Uncle said. "We must make sure the prince is satisfied with his visit. We all know that the bandit threat gets worse every year that we don't have royal protection."

The priest, Ki Sardu, cleared his throat. "I believe

the possibility of a marriage was discussed with the messenger yesterday," he said to Big Uncle.

Big Uncle nodded. His smile shone nearly as bright as his oiled forehead.

"Don't get me wrong, Citra is a fine girl," the priest continued. "Yet doesn't it seem rather ... unlikely? A prince marrying a village girl?"

"Not at all," Bapak Iya jumped in. "Don't you remember the old Bhre Mataram took that girl from Salatiga as a wife all those years ago? Not a first wife, granted, but a wife all the same, and a good thing for Salatiga it was too. They don't have nearly the trouble with bandits that we do."

"Perhaps our *juru kunci* might have some insight into this matter," Big Uncle said, turning to the ancient seer.

There was a long silence. Kancil was beginning to think the *juru kunci* might actually be asleep this time when finally he raised his head and gazed into the middle distance. "The spirits," he said, "have nothing to say on the matter."

"Well then," said Big Uncle, "tomorrow we should get to work rebuilding the *joglo*. It would not do for the prince to arrive and have nowhere to stay." He started to rise, pausing when he realised that the *juru kunci* hadn't finished speaking.

"A royal wedding might bring wealth to this village,

but it will not bring back the temple treasures," the *juru kunci* said.

There was an awkward silence as the other three men looked at each other, none wanting to be the first to speak. Finally, Bapak Iya spoke up. "A royal match can't be a *bad* thing, though. Can it?" he asked hopefully.

"No, of course not. You're right of course," Big Uncle blustered. "And, er, forgive me," he inclined his head towards the *juru kunci*, "but after all these years, I'm afraid we must accept that the temple treasures are lost forever."

"Perhaps," said the *juru kunci*, quietly.

7

MOTHER

The news of the prince's visit threw Big Uncle's household into a frenzy of preparation and within a week Kancil and Mother had slipped into a routine. They rose each day before sunrise and Kancil would cut a lime for Mother to suck on to treat her cough. The treatment wasn't working but Mother waved away Kancil's concern saying, "It's the inland air. I'll be fine once the rains stop."

Mother spent her day weaving with Big Aunt and Citra in the pavilion at the front of the house while Kancil worked in the kitchen. Before Bibi came in to start ordering her about, she lit the fire, swept out the hut and sprinkled the floor with water to settle the dust. While she was doing this, Kitchen Boy would arrive with the day's rice for her to prepare. Apparently, it wasn't in his nature to walk in the door and announce himself like a normal person. Instead he had to sneak in and find a different hiding place to leap from each day. The first time Kancil screamed and dropped the watering bucket on the floor, leaving a muddy patch that resulted in her first proper beating from Bibi. The second time she screamed but managed to hold onto the bucket. The third time she hit him with the bucket. He laughed every time.

Once she had hulled the rice and put it in the steamer, Kancil would spend the rest of her morning bent over a pan of spitting coconut oil or grinding spice paste or picking bugs out of *kangkung* leaves. When the rice was ready, Bibi would divide it up. A portion of rice with greens was set on a tray for the weavers in the pavilion; a bigger portion with greens and dried fish was for Big Uncle and the men repairing the *joglo* where the prince would stay. Bibi and Ida kept a portion for themselves, with whatever greens and fish they could hold back from the others without questions being asked. Kancil and Kitchen Boy got the scrapings from the steaming basket.

When Mother returned with the leftovers from the weaving pavilion, Bibi and Ida would grab the tray and return to their position on the daybed. This was the cue for Kitchen Boy to stretch out on the ground and for Mother and Kancil to walk around the tamarind tree to their shack, to shelter from the midday heat. The sound of Bibi rapping at the iron pot with her cane was the signal to go back to work. The afternoon proceeded in much the same way as the morning, except that Kancil got to leave the yard with Ida for a short time to bathe and collect the washing.

In the evenings, Mother would dress in her good *kain* and walk to the pavilion to continue Citra's lessons. Kancil spent her evenings waiting on the men in the *pendopo*. It wasn't such a bad job – mostly she sat near the fence, listening to the men's conversation and waiting for Big Uncle to clap his hands and call "tamarind" or "ginger".

On her second night at the *pendopo* she was startled by something in a nearby tree. At first she thought it was a forest cat, stretched out along a branch, but when she looked more closely she realised it was Kitchen Boy grinning down at her.

She never saw him climb up or down the tree but he was there every night. Kancil would hear a soft thud as she collected the empty gourds and cups from the *pendopo* – just the kind of sound a forest cat would make leaping from a tree – and Kitchen Boy would be behind her. He slept in the *pendopo* at night. "By order of Bapak Thani, Big Uncle to you," he told her one time. "So you can rest easy knowing that I am protecting the household from a tiger attack through the front gate."

One night, Kitchen Boy followed Kancil into the kitchen when she went to put away the dishes. She braced herself for a practical joke. Instead, he went straight to the heavy grinding stone that was used to prepare *jamu* ingredients and shook a small parcel of bark and seeds onto it.

"Stoke the fire and get the water boiling while I grind these," he said. There was an uncharacteristic seriousness in his voice. Perplexed, Kancil did as she was told.

Kitchen Boy tipped the powdered ingredients into a small clay pot and motioned for Kancil to pour the boiled water over the powder. "This is for your mother's cough," he said, handing her the pot and a cup. "These have to be back on the shelf before Bibi arrives in the morning or your life won't be worth living," he added.

Mother's rasping cough and the dark circles under her eyes had been getting worse ever since they arrived in the village, but Kancil had let herself believe Mother when she said the damp air was the cause. Now Kancil felt ashamed. She should have paid more attention.

After that night, making *jamu* for Mother became part of Kancil and Kitchen Boy's routine. Kancil didn't know where he got the ingredients or why he was being so kind, but Mother said it was making her feel better. Kancil wasn't convinced that she was coughing any less but she told herself she just noticed it more because Kitchen Boy had made her realise it was serious.

The midday rest was Kancil's favourite time of day. Usually Mother managed to hide a little parcel of leftover greens in the folds of her *kain* and Kancil would eat them up greedily before stretching out on the bamboo platform in their shack. It wasn't the food, though, that made this time of day special. Their shack was far enough away from the kitchen and the house for them to talk quietly without being overheard, and the chickens next door always warned them if someone was coming down the passageway or from the kitchen.

"Why did Bibi call me 'bandit spawn'?" Kancil whispered the first time she dared to speak.

"Don't pay any attention to her, she's jealous," said Mother. "Her life hasn't turned out well and she takes out her bitterness on anyone she thinks is weaker than her."

"But why 'bandit spawn'?" Kancil wasn't going to let her mother change the subject.

"The forests around here are full of bandits," said Mother. "If someone doesn't have a father, it's an easy insult to say their father was a bandit. Don't listen to her, child. Nobody else does."

Each day Kancil coaxed a little more information

about the past from Mother. She found out that her parents had met in the village when Father visited to sell frankincense. Mataram was different in those days; pilgrims came from far away to meditate at the great forest temples nearby. Where pilgrims went, traders followed and for a while the village did very well from the passing traffic. But where there is pilgrim gold, bandits are never far away.

"The prince, the *old* Bhre Mataram, kept soldiers here," said Mother. "They helped keep things in order and the prince would reward them each harvest season when he visited. One year, the year your father came here, the prince didn't visit. The soldiers grew tired of waiting for their wages and abandoned their duties. Nobody knew then that the old Bhre had died, but knowing *why* he hadn't visited wouldn't have made any difference.

"Some very bad things happened. You don't need to know the details. Your father wasn't involved but people stopped trusting the Sunda merchants and there was no way I would have been allowed to marry him. When Mbah Merapi began to fume, the *juru kunci* warned us that he meant to destroy the village. It was a terrible thing to happen, but it gave us the opportunity to get away in the confusion."

Kancil was shocked. "You and Father *eloped*?" she whispered.

"*Tsk!*" said Mother. "You make it sound like a scandal. It wasn't like that; it was ... complicated. That's all I'll say about the matter so don't bother asking me any more. Digging up the past won't do any good." Mother began to cough, so Kancil let the subject drop.

Whenever Kancil couldn't sleep, her mind drifted back to that moment in the *pondok* when she thought she heard her father whispering to her. Every time she tried to remember the scene the same thing happened – she strained her ears to hear his voice, but all she could hear was a rushing noise, like the wind in the trees or the sound inside a seashell. Then the image of her necklace sinking into the mud would appear before her eyes.

At that point she would shake herself out of the daydream; she certainly didn't want to remember *that* moment. But one day she let the image stay. All but three shells had vanished into the mud. As each of the last three shells sank, a thought burned brightly in Kancil's mind: the scoundrel, the temple treasure, Agus.

She sat up, gasping. I must have fallen asleep, she thought. It was just a dream and hearing Father's voice was my mind playing tricks because I've got nobody to talk to. The scoundrel is best forgotten, the temple treasure is none of my business and Agus ...

Kancil couldn't think of a reason why her brother

would appear in the same dream as the scoundrel and the temple treasure.

Could Father be telling her that the scoundrel and the temple treasure were the keys to finding Agus? Make up your mind, she scolded herself. Is it Father's voice or my imagination? A part of her didn't want to believe that Father's spirit was talking to her because that would surely mean he was dead. On the other hand, if Father's spirit was trying to guide her to Agus, then that meant her brother must still be alive.

A loud *tok-eh* broke the midday silence. If a gecko called *tok-eh* nine times, Kancil always made a wish. She counted each call … six, seven, eight … The gap between each call grew longer and longer; geckoes hardly ever made it to nine. *Tok-eeeeh.* The final call was a drawn-out sigh. Kancil looked up at the thatch. The gecko was staring down at her. "Send me someone to talk to," she whispered. The gecko turned tail and vanished.

The next morning Bibi decided that Kancil should take over the laundry from Ida. To Kancil, leaving the kitchen and joining the circle of girls and women at the washing pool felt like being released from prison. Best of all, Ibu Tari was there; the kind old lady she had met on her first day in the village.

"Does she not speak at all?" one of the girls asked Ida when they reached the pool.

Ida shrugged. "Apparently not. It's her foolish mother's fault. She brought a curse upon herself by leaving here in the first place. Now she's come crawling back with no husband and an idiot daughter for company, and she expects her family to welcome her with open arms." Ida snorted. "She'll be lucky."

Fortunately, Ida left as soon as she had shown Kancil where the family's washing stone was.

When Kancil waded into the river, the girls in the washing circle looked at each other. Nobody wanted to stand next to a curse. Ibu Tari motioned for the girls beside her to make room and she welcomed Kancil with a warm smile. Following Ibu Tari's lead, the girls around her nodded in greeting and some even smiled shyly.

"She's got funny eyes," said one of the younger girls. "Look, they're the colour of teak wood. They're not like normal eyes at all."

"I think they're pretty," said another. "I wonder if she sees the same way out of them as we do. Maybe colours look different to her."

"Really, Hen. You come up with the strangest ideas," said Ibu Tari. "Now leave her alone; you're embarrassing her."

The group gathered around the flat slab of rock at the

water's edge and gossiped openly about Citra and Big Aunt. Kancil was reassured to discover that they weren't well liked. The girls showed no further interest in her though; without a voice to join in with the gossip she was invisible here, just as she was invisible at the *pendopo* in the evenings and in the kitchen – except when she did something wrong.

"Do you think the prince will marry her?" a girl asked as she slapped a sodden *kain* onto the rock and began pummelling it with her washing stone.

"Who?" asked one of her companions.

"Citra. My father says the prince's messenger told Bapak Thani that the prince is looking for a wife and the spirits told the *juru kunci* the prince is going to choose Citra."

"Well, fancy that. Poor thing," said Ibu Tari.

"Who? The prince or Citra?"

At this the whole group laughed loudly and splashed the speaker. The washing was forgotten. "Back to work girls!" Ibu Tari scolded, but she smiled. "You should feel sorry for them both," she continued. "Citra would be a handful to be sure, but being married to a prince would not be easy."

The girls' faces showed that they didn't believe this last remark. Ibu Tari sighed. "You don't think a member of the royal family is going to take a silly village girl as his first wife, do you? Marrying Citra would be a convenient way for him to show he's serious about being Prince of Mataram, get us on side and happy to give him a generous share of the harvest. Bapak Thani gets status, Ibu Thani gets some more gold to hang around her neck. I don't see that Citra gets much out of it, though."

Kancil listened as the gossip continued around her. It wasn't quite the same thing as having someone to talk to but at least it was talk, not the barked commands and flying cooking implements that served as communication with Bibi. Kitchen Boy had learned some of her sign language but he didn't make conversation, he played games.

The girls' talk was all about the prince – about the *joglo* the men were building for him to stay in and the progress of repairs to the village *pendopo* at the north gate where the prince would be welcomed with dance and *gamelan* music.

Ibu Tari was responsible for teaching the young girls the steps of the welcome dance. The girls' attention was wholly focussed on Ibu Tari, trying to tease information from her about who would be in the front row of the dance.

"It's a lucky thing Bapak Thani's sister came back when she did," Ibu Tari said, trying to change the subject. "You should see the weaving she is doing for the *joglo* furnishings – she must have learned a thing or two in Lawucilik."

"My mother said she was supposed to marry the person we don't talk about and she ran away to Lawucilik because she knew—" one of the girls began.

Ibu Tari cut her off. "That's enough idle talk," she said, looking around in alarm. "You know voices carry on the water."

8

KANCIL SPEAKS

Kancil couldn't wait to get back to the sleeping shack after her midday meal. She was sure that the scoundrel and "the person we don't talk about" were the same man and she was determined to get some answers from the only person she was able to ask. As she walked from the kitchen she grew impatient with how slowly Mother was moving and skipped ahead of her.

"Why are you so energetic today?" asked Mother as she eased herself onto the bed.

"I went to the washing pool today," Kancil whispered back. "They were all praising your weaving."

"Is that so?" asked Mother. "That's nice."

Kancil was too excited to hear the weariness in her voice. "They said something interesting too about someone you were supposed to marry," she continued.

Mother was quiet for a moment, then she said, "You shouldn't listen to common people's gossip."

"*Common* people?"

"Yes, *common* people. You've no business listening to washerwomen's chitchat. Our family is above that sort of nonsense."

Kancil couldn't believe her ears. "*Our* family?" she gasped. "You mean my snooty aunt who insults you at every opportunity and treats me like dirt, and my halfwit cousin who can't manage even the simplest sentence in polite Jawa?"

"Be grateful you have a home, and leave the past where it is," Mother growled. "You'll get a slap if you answer back again." With that, she turned away angrily.

Kancil was silent but fury bubbled up inside her. She desperately needed to scream. When the rhythmic breathing beside her told her that Mother was asleep, she carefully rolled off the bed. Without knowing where she was going, she let her feet carry her along the path to the bathing pool. Kancil was used to the sounds of laughter and splashing water echoing off the rocks and trees that skirted the pool. But that was in the early morning or the late afternoon. Now the sun was beating down from its highest point, baking the rocks and dazzling her as it reflected off the still water.

She stood at the water's edge, listening. The silence of the bathing pool amplified the eerie screeches of birds and monkeys in the forest on the opposite riverbank, but the sounds were few and far between. Like the villagers, the animals were conserving their energy in the midday heat.

This was the first time she had been properly alone for many months and suddenly she was hit by a wave of self-pity. Thoughts of Agus and Father leaped into her mind and the tears that she had managed to hold back for so long flowed unchecked. Kancil rubbed at her eyes angrily. What is the point in crying? she asked herself. For someone like Citra it's a way to get what she wants but it's not going to do *you* any good.

One thing was for certain, she thought. If Agus were here, she wouldn't still be standing on the edge of the pool. They would have raced into the water, daring each other to dive deeper and deeper. "Inland people don't swim," Mother had warned the first day they came to the bathing pool, and since then Kancil had been careful not to dive under the water. Now she was alone it was too tempting.

She unwound her *kain* and bundled it up, placing a large, flat river stone on top to secure it. Then, she bounded into the water before she had time to think. The water was cool and it soothed her hot skin, but the lonely, still pool was a poor substitute for the playful waves at home.

Kancil stepped further into the pool until she couldn't touch the bottom. She duck dived and swam down until her outstretched hand touched a slimy rock. She tumble-turned and crouched on the bottom. "Where are you, Agus?" she yelled with all her might. She watched as her voice was carried to the surface as a mass of air bubbles. Springing off the rocks, she kicked as hard as she could and broke the surface to take a huge gulp of air.

A shape caught her eye as she shook water out of her ears. Kancil gasped. Kitchen Boy was standing on the riverbank, holding her clothes in his good hand, and grinning. "I know you can talk," he said. "I'll give you your clothes back if you ask nicely." Kancil treaded water and glared at him. He was bluffing; he couldn't possibly have heard her. She pursed her lips and shook her head.

"That won't work," he said, smiling his crooked smile. He squinted up at the sky. The sun was dipping towards the trees and a thick thunderous cloud was rising up to meet it. "And if you don't get out, the water spirit will pull you under," he added. "She will wake up soon and rain makes her hungry."

Kancil could see that she was trapped, but the

mention of the water spirit had given her an idea. "Please," she whispered. Kitchen Boy's grin widened in victory. He placed her clothes at his feet. "Turn around," she hissed. Kitchen Boy coloured slightly and did as he was told.

Scrambling out of the water, Kancil whipped her *kain* around her body. She tugged at Kitchen Boy's arm and motioned for him to follow her a little way off the path into the bamboo.

"I can't speak," she whispered, looking around and crouching behind the trees.

"Why are you talking strangely?" he asked.

"*Sssshhhh!*" she whispered. "If I speak in my normal voice, the mountain spirits will hear me." She pulled him down beside her and continued to whisper into his ear. "When the mountain near my village breathed fire, I bargained with the spirits to spare my mother's life. In return I had to agree never to speak again."

"Why?" asked Kitchen Boy. Kancil had thought her story was quite good but Kitchen Boy didn't seem impressed. He acted the fool but perhaps he was smarter than she had thought. It frustrated her that people treated her like she was half-witted because she didn't speak, but until now it hadn't occurred to her that she did the same to Kitchen Boy.

Kancil turned to her last resort: she pinned him to a

94

tree with all her weight and pinched his arm as hard as she could. "I don't know why," she growled, "but if you tell anyone that I can speak, it will bring the mountain spirits here for sure and then you will be responsible for whatever happens next."

At that moment a flash of lightning lit the sky, then seconds later a deafening peal of thunder cracked in the treetops. The smell of lightning-singed timber filled Kancil's nostrils and her skin prickled with thunder-jitters. Maybe the spirits didn't take kindly to her making up stories about them.

Kitchen Boy shook her off and rubbed at his arm. An ugly red welt blazed where she had pinched him. "The thing is," he said, "I thought your father and brother were swallowed by the earth, not eaten by mountain fire."

"Ye-es," replied Kancil. How could she make such a stupid mistake? "That happened before the mountain breathed fire," she said, thinking fast. "That's why I had to bargain with the spirits. Mother was all I had left."

Another flash of lightning lit the sky but the thunder was moving away. Kitchen Boy nodded thoughtfully. "Good enough for the yokels round here to believe," he said. "Doesn't convince me, of course."

"Why not?" Kancil asked.

"Well … mountain spirits, water spirits. They're all

just made up stories to stop children from running away or jumping in the river. Now there's a thing – you can swim. What's that all about? And you do talk strangely. You're not from round here, are you?"

"You really don't believe in the spirits?" Kancil gasped. She wasn't trying to change the subject; she was genuinely shocked.

"*Real* spirits, yes, absolutely. Why wouldn't I believe what I've seen with my own eyes? But not the silly children's story type. A *real* spirit wouldn't waste its time bargaining with some girl to save her mother's life, believe me."

"You've *seen* a spirit? When? How?"

"Tell me where you're really from and I'll tell you about the spirits," Kitchen Boy answered.

Kancil shook her head and crossed her arms.

"Oh, well," Kitchen Boy said, "looks like we'll both have to stay curious. Come on, we'd better get back before we're missed."

"You won't tell on me?" Kancil whispered as she followed him out of the bamboo grove.

Kitchen Boy turned and grinned at her. "Of course I won't tell," he laughed. "Who would believe me?"

As he was about to step onto the path, Kancil tugged at his *sarung*. "Will you tell me one thing?" she whispered.

"Maybe," he replied, his eyes narrowing.

"Do you know who the scoundrel is?"

Kitchen Boy shrugged. "The temple forests are teeming with scoundrels," he said.

"There's one in particular. They call him 'the scoundrel' or 'the person we don't talk about'."

"Oh, *that* scoundrel," said Kitchen Boy, nodding wisely. "The thing about the scoundrel we don't talk about is that nobody talks about him so nobody knows who he is." His eyes were sparkling with glee, clearly enjoying his own joke. Kancil tried to hide her irritation, knowing that it would only encourage him.

The dream, or vision, or whatever it was, about Agus, the scoundrel and the temple treasure had continued to nag her. She knew she would get no peace until she worked out what it meant.

"Do you think my Small Aunt would know?" she asked.

"Maybe."

"Do you think you could arrange for me to see her?"

Kitchen Boy breathed out through his nostrils in mock exasperation. "I think I liked you better when you were mute," he said. "You weren't nearly so demanding."

"Please," said Kancil. "It's important."

"Why?"

Kancil imitated Kitchen Boy's mock exasperation.

"I think I liked *you* better when I was mute," she said. "You didn't ask nearly so many questions."

Kitchen Boy laughed heartily at this. "I'll see what I can do," he said.

9
RETURN TO THE BANYAN TREE

Kitchen Boy didn't expose Kancil's secret. He even stopped jumping out to frighten her when she was sweeping the floor and he didn't tease her the way he used to. Kancil found herself almost missing the old Kitchen Boy – at least his practical jokes would have distracted her from worrying about Mother. Her cough was getting worse, she barely slept at night, her hair was going grey. The hair would have seemed trivial except that Mother had once made Kancil promise that if she ever spotted a grey hair on her head, she would pull it out. Mother had so many grey hairs now that she would be half-bald if Kancil were to pluck them.

Word had come that the prince would arrive at the new moon. As that date drew closer, the working days grew longer. Mother stayed strapped to the loom until she could barely see the threads. For Kancil, the pleasure of drinking young coconut juice, once her favourite drink, was lost. The smell reminded her of the hours she spent grazing her knuckles on the coconut grater or bent over the smoky fire, turning the coconut flesh into oil. It was all she could do to limp back to the shack and heave herself onto the platform to sleep in the middle of the day.

Three days before the new moon, all the gourds of oil and sacks of grain were lined up along the kitchen wall, ready to be taken to the *joglo* kitchen. Kancil was sitting on her low stool by the fire, barely awake, when a booming voice jolted her back to the present. "All right, Bibi. What have you got for us?" Kancil recognised that voice – it was Bapak Pohon, the giant who had terrified her on her first day in the village.

"Little chicken!" the giant bellowed when he saw her. A wide smile lit up his face. The giant's smile faltered for a moment as he drew close enough to see Kancil's bare legs and arms, marked by the bruises from Bibi's beatings and the cuts and burns of everyday kitchen life. He quickly recovered and reached down to squeeze her shoulder. "Ah, little chicken, it's good to see you again. I've just seen the beautiful cloths your mother made for the *joglo*. Wah! Such fine work! And here you are, keeping the kitchen going. Where would we be without you two? You must have been sent by the gods!"

Kancil heard Ida snorting in the shadows. It hardly registered. Tears sprang to her eyes in response to Bapak Pohon's kind words and she hung her head, confused and embarrassed, hoping he would go away – it was so much simpler to be ignored.

"Bapak Pohon! Bapak Pohon!" Bibi called to the giant. "Stop bothering the kitchen girl and get your men in order." As she spoke, she took a swipe at a young man who was reaching for the last gourd on the bench. "Don't take that one, idiot, that's to stay here. Just because he's a prince doesn't mean he gets everything."

The giant sighed, then winked at Kancil and patted her cheek. Kancil wiped her eyes and looked around to find some way to busy herself. Kitchen Boy was squatting on the floor nearby, rocking on his heels and grinning at her like a maniac. Kancil knew that look. It meant he was up to something.

"Bibi," Bapak Pohon said, "I need to talk to you about a delicate matter." He drew her away to the other end of the kitchen but his voice was loud enough for Kancil to hear. "Particular *jamu* preparations are needed to make sure a certain someone is looking and feeling her best when the prince arrives," he said, "but you know what Ibu Jamu is like."

"I don't see what it's got to do with me," Bibi sniffed.

"Well …" said Bapak Pohon, "we all know Ibu Jamu

has a soft spot for the boy," at this he nodded in Kitchen Boy's direction, "and the girl, well, she is kin after all."

Kancil realised that Ibu Jamu was Small Aunt. She held her breath – was this what Kitchen Boy was grinning about?

"Get to your point," Bibi snapped. "I haven't got all day."

Bapak Pohon cleared his throat. "Bapak Thani and I were wondering if it might be possible for you to spare the two of them tomorrow so they could visit Ibu Jamu and, er, acquire the relevant ingredients."

"Hmpf," said Bibi. "If that's the case, why didn't you come out and say it straightaway? If Bapak Thani wants them to go traipsing off to that witch's lair, who am I to say no?" She stabbed at the dirt floor with her cane.

"You're a good woman, Bibi," said Bapak Pohon. "I'm sure you will be rewarded one day for all your good work." He looked over Bibi's head to Kitchen Boy and winked.

That night, Mother sipped at Kitchen Boy's *jamu* as usual. Kancil felt she was doing it only to be polite. Her illness was more powerful than his simple remedy. "I'll be better soon," she said. "The cloths are all ready for the *joglo* so tomorrow I can rest." She lay down but the coughing started again so she propped herself up.

It must be Father's spirit that is directing my

thoughts, Kancil decided. Maybe the scoundrel and the temple treasure aren't really important. Father just put the thought of them into my head to make me want to see Small Aunt because he knew I needed Small Aunt's knowledge of *jamu* to save Mother.

The image of the three shells from her necklace slipping into the mud still nagged: the scoundrel, the temple treasure, Agus. Why would her father taunt her with the hope of finding Agus if that wasn't the reason for presenting her with the puzzle?

Mother was looking at her. "You should sleep, child," she said. "Now the rains have come you will have to cross the river further to the north. It will be a long walk to your aunt's home."

Kancil couldn't sleep. In her mind, wheels kept turning: Agus is alive – somewhere; the treasure is not lost – perhaps; the scoundrel is … who is the scoundrel? Mother and Small Aunt know so that should be the easy part of the puzzle to solve.

She could tell Mother was awake and finally she gave up on sleep herself and sat up, gazing out at the dark shape of the tamarind tree. Mother reached for her hand and stroked it gently. "I made your uncle promise that when I'm gone he will take care of you," she said. "You have a home here."

All Kancil could do was shake her head. I will not let

my mother die, she thought to herself. I will leave this place and I will find a way to make her come with me and we will find Agus.

The next morning Kancil was more worried than ever about Mother. She had been coughing all night and her breathing was ragged.

Kancil lit the kitchen fire before dawn as she did every morning, but when Kitchen Boy arrived he wasn't carrying the usual measure of rice. Instead he was carrying a *kendi* that was still wet from the well. "Are you ready then?" he asked cheerfully. Kancil wiped her eyes and shoved at a piece of firewood that was sticking out of the stove, keeping her back to him for a moment while she collected herself.

"What's up with you?" Kitchen Boy asked. "I thought you *wanted* to walk halfway up the mountain to visit your crazy aunt!"

"Mother is sick," Kancil signed.

"I know," he replied.

"She's *really* sick."

"I did my best." Kitchen Boy sounded hurt.

"I know."

Kancil followed Kitchen Boy down the side of the house to the front courtyard. She was surprised to see her uncle's feet poking out over the edge of the weaving pavilion when they walked by. A snore loud enough to make the pavilion's corner posts rattle told her why he wasn't sleeping in the house. She exchanged glances with Kitchen Boy and allowed herself a small smile in reply to his snickering.

Mother will be all right until I get back and Small Aunt will give me the right *jamu* to cure her, Kancil told herself as they passed through the quiet village.

The *pendopo* by the north gate had a new roof and smelled of freshly cut timber. Beyond the village, the fields that had been empty dirt bowls when she arrived were now awash with tender green rice shoots. Somehow, though, the hopefulness of everything around her made Kancil feel even more hopeless.

As they passed the *pondok* where she and Mother had sheltered from the rain, Kancil thought about her necklace buried in the mud. She felt a powerful urge to climb under the floor and dig it out but she resisted. It will be safe there, she told herself.

She paused to gaze at the temples. The bell-shaped top of the tallest spire was silhouetted against the dawn sky.

"Have you been there?" she whispered.

Kitchen Boy nodded. He put the *kendi* on the ground to give his arm a rest.

"What are they like?"

"Mostly ruins," he said. "There are trees and vines growing all over and through them. You can still see the carvings though, on the walls, and some of them have statues inside."

"Mother told me that ceremonies are held there."

"Really?" said Kitchen Boy. "That must have been a long time ago. Nobody from the village goes there now. Those temples are bad luck."

"*You've* been there, though."

"Yes. I don't need luck. I've got my tiger spirit to protect me. Anyway, if I'm out in the forest when a thunderstorm comes, I'd rather trust my luck taking shelter in a cursed temple than under a tree." He picked up the *kendi* and set off on the path to the mountain once more. "Come on," he said.

"Ibu Jamu, Ibu Jamu," Kitchen Boy called softly through the high fenceposts of Small Aunt's orchard. They waited. Kitchen Boy tapped on the fence and called out again, then retreated to the shade of the banyan tree, settled himself against the trunk and closed his eyes.

"Shouldn't we go in?" Kancil whispered. "I don't think she heard you."

Kitchen Boy opened one eye. "She heard," he said, "and even if she didn't, we couldn't go in." He shut his eyes again.

Kancil could tell that he was waiting for her to ask him why they couldn't go in, but she resisted – her head was full of worry for Mother and she didn't feel like playing Kitchen Boy's game. In any case, Mother had told her about the holy woman. They sat in silence for a time then Kitchen Boy gave a loud sigh of exasperation. "All right, you win," he said. "We can't go in because your aunt is a servant in the home of a lady who has taken a vow to retreat from the world and nobody may see her except your aunt."

"Why?"

"Why what?"

"Why did she retreat from the world?"

Kitchen Boy thought for a moment. "I don't know," he said finally with a shrug. "It's the sort of thing ladies do, isn't it, if things don't work out for them in the world?"

Kancil snorted. "Sounds stupid to me," she said.

Kitchen Boy frowned. "Isn't that what's happened to you?" he asked.

"What do you mean?"

"I'd hardly call the occasional secret conversation with a lame kitchen boy being out in the world. You're pretty much confined to the kitchen for the rest–" He stopped himself, too late. "Sorry."

"Well," Kancil said, straightening her back, "I'm

going to take it as a compliment that you're comparing me to a proper lady."

"That's the spirit," said Kitchen Boy.

"And for your information, I don't intend to be confined to Bibi's kitchen for the rest of my life." Kancil regretted speaking as soon as the words left her mouth. She didn't want Kitchen Boy to ask her how she planned to escape. That would force her to admit that she didn't have the slightest idea. She quickly changed the subject to distract him.

"Are you not even curious to know who the lady is or why she retreated from the world?"

Kitchen Boy put his head to one side. "I've never really thought about it," he said. "I guess that seems strange to you but to me she's just always been there. She's related to the old Bhre Mataram somehow. She came here before I was born and nobody talks much about the past, so I don't know any more."

"What about your parents?" Kancil asked. "Don't you ever wonder who they were?"

"No." Kitchen Boy shrugged dismissively. "Whoever they were, they abandoned me. Why should I care?"

Kancil gazed towards the orchard hidden behind the high fence. I guess I'll never know either, she thought.

10

IBU JAMU

The sun was high in the sky and Kancil was wilting in the heat. Her head nodded forwards and she dozed. She was jerked back into wakefulness by a voice.

"Why did you come here?" Small Aunt was standing in front of her.

Kancil scrambled to bow before her as Kitchen Boy was doing.

"My dear, good Aunt. Your brother, the Bapak Thani, has sent us to beg that you be so kind as to spare a small portion of your highly esteemed *jamu* for the sake of the continued prosperity of the village and all its inhabitants," she recited, allowing just enough of a whine to enter her voice to sound properly subservient.

She had practised her speech on the way from the village. Kitchen Boy had coached her with her local accent. The smattering of polite language was her own idea and she felt a little proud at how impressed he was. Now she raised her head ever so slightly to see what impression she had made on her aunt.

Small Aunt was wearing much the same expression as when they first met – the expression that made Kancil feel like a piece of inferior cloth. "I see you gave up on pretending to be mute," Small Aunt said.

Kitchen Boy sat up and brushed the dirt off his knees. "Oh no," he said. "With everyone else she's as silent as a washing stone. I'm the only one who knows. It's a pity really because she does a great impersonation of Citra and I'm the only one who gets to appreciate it."

Kancil glared at Kitchen Boy. She had gone to all that trouble to win Small Aunt over with her polite language and he went and ruined it with his usual crassness. Her irritation turned to confusion when she saw that Small Aunt's eyes were shining, then resentment as she realised that her own performance was part of the joke, that she was the only one taking this seriously. She swallowed her pride, reminding herself that she needed Small Aunt's help to make Mother well again.

"Perhaps I misjudged you," Small Aunt said to her. "At least you've chosen your friends wisely." She nodded her head towards Kitchen Boy. "Does your mother know you've spoken to him?"

Kancil shook her head. "Mother is very sick," she said. "She needs your *jamu*."

Small Aunt was immediately serious, quizzing Kancil about Mother's symptoms and Kitchen Boy about the treatment he had given her. "I'll do what I can," she said, "but I can't imagine my oaf of a brother sent you to get *jamu* for my sister. What does *he* want?"

Kitchen Boy explained that because Kancil wanted to ask Small Aunt about the scoundrel he had come up with the idea of getting Big Uncle to send them for *jamu* for Citra.

"Why do you want to know about the scoundrel?" Small Aunt asked Kancil.

Kancil shrugged. "I don't really know," she said. "It seemed important for some reason but I don't think it is now. I just need *jamu* to cure Mother." She was feeling terribly tired all of a sudden. All she could think about was how lifeless Mother had looked propped up in their rickety shack that morning. The scoundrel, the temple treasure, they weren't important. And Agus must wait, she told herself.

"Well," said Small Aunt, "there's no need for me to tell you about the scoundrel then. I'll go and get your *jamu* and you can be on your way."

"Actually," said Kitchen Boy, "I'd quite like to know about him."

"Why?"

"Because nobody who knows anything wants to talk about him and that's made me curious," he said.

"Bring four loads of firewood to the orchard gate and I will bring you *jamu* and the truth," said Small Aunt. Then she stood up and walked briskly towards the orchard.

"Come on," Kitchen Boy said to Kancil, "I know a place upstream where broken trees wash up after the big rains. She didn't say it had to be *dry* firewood."

Kancil and Kitchen Boy stacked the last of the logs against the fence as the rain started falling. They scurried under the shelter of the banyan tree, where they found Small Aunt waiting for them. As well as the promised *jamu* she had brought a pot of hot ginger tea, which she poured into small clay cups.

"Tell me what you know about the scoundrel," said Small Aunt.

That didn't seem very fair, Kancil thought. Her job was to collect firewood – it was Small Aunt who was supposed to be doing the storytelling. But she wasn't in a position to argue. "I heard you mention him once," she said slowly, "and Big Uncle said something about rebuilding after ... well, I don't know what, but it seemed to have something to do with the scoundrel. And then one of the girls at the washing pool said that Mother was supposed to marry someone. She didn't say the scoundrel but I think that's who she was talking about. She said Mother ran away from the village because she knew something. That's all I know."

"You have been listening carefully, haven't you?" said Small Aunt, placing her empty cup on the ground and motioning for Kancil to refill it. Kitchen Boy gulped down the last of his tea and dived to place his cup under the teapot in Kancil's hands.

"Manners, Tiger Boy," said Small Aunt gently. Kancil bristled at how Kitchen Boy got away with behaviour that would earn her a slap at the very least. Up to a point it was to be expected – he was a boy after all – but Small Aunt treated him like a pet to be indulged, rather than a real boy, and at Big Uncle's house he was able to come and go as he pleased. It almost felt as though people were a little afraid of him. Everyone except Bibi, of course. She was afraid of nobody.

Small Aunt took a sip of tea and cleared her throat. "There was a man – well, a boy really – whom your mother was promised to marry," she said. "Nobody knew he was the scoundrel then of course, though I must say I never thought much of him. Your mother certainly didn't run away because she knew something, though. She left because she met your father and he filled her head with all sorts of nonsense about the sea."

Kancil glanced nervously at Kitchen Boy. Perhaps she should have let Small Aunt know that her Sunda origins were still a secret. Kitchen Boy was lying on his back with his eyes half-closed. He didn't seem to be paying much attention.

"The scoundrel did a terrible thing. He brought a curse on the village and he was banished. That's all there is to tell."

Kitchen Boy was sitting up straight in an instant. "*That* was not four loads of firewood worth of truth," he said. Kancil was glad now that he could get away with saying the things he did.

"All right," Small Aunt sighed. She held out her cup for more tea. "It began with a rumour about a place in the forest that rang with laughter all night. The scoundrel and his friends had comfortable lives – they were the sons of important men in the village, so their duties were light. At night when everybody else fell asleep in exhaustion, they had energy to burn and curiosity about the forest laughter.

"One thing led to another," she continued. "At first they dared each other to creep further and further into the forest. When they found the bandits' gambling den, they kept their distance, watching and listening, learning the rules of the strange dice games they saw being played in the firelight. Soon they were playing their own games in a different part of the forest.

"The scoundrel was a clever dice player and eventually his friends grew tired of losing to him so they found other things to do. But the scoundrel wanted to keep playing. One night I saw him venture further into the forest and enter the bandits' circle of firelight and laughter."

Kancil couldn't help herself. "You were in the forest at night?" she gasped.

"Yes," Small Aunt snapped. "What of it? I was apprenticed to the *jamu* maker. Some *jamu* ingredients are more potent if they are gathered at night. Now do you want to know about the scoundrel or not?"

Kancil nodded meekly.

"The scoundrel was a good gambler but he wasn't good enough to beat the *Sunda* bandits." She shot Kancil a meaningful look. Out of the corner of her eye, Kancil saw Kitchen Boy stir. He was staring at her, his lips curling into a victorious grin.

Small Aunt continued, unaware of the secret she had just revealed. "Things started going missing, jewellery mostly. At first people blamed mischievous spirits but the spirits don't keep what they steal – they might break things or put them back in a different place but they always return them. So people started blaming travellers. There were many of them in the village in those days; the pilgrims who came to visit the forest temples and the traders who followed them, selling them things they didn't know they needed. Your father was one of those.

"So it wasn't a good time to be a travelling merchant – nobody would ever accuse a pilgrim. Yet, even when the less trustworthy traders had been hounded out of the village and those remaining were being watched like snakes, the thefts continued.

"Finally, when there was no more gold or silver in the village, the unthinkable happened – the forest temples were plundered. It took the priests a while to realise what was happening because the precious talismans were kept hidden and only brought out for special ceremonies. The golden holy water bowl was the only one that was used regularly and one day, after a ceremony, it vanished. The priests checked the other treasures' hiding places and discovered the awful truth.

"The ceremony had been to appease the mountain, Mbah Merapi, who had been rumbling and smoking for some time. As soon as the thefts were discovered, the *juru kunci* went straight to his secret place to meditate, hoping that he could placate Mbah Merapi. On his way back through the forest he saw the scoundrel handing the golden bowl over to the bandit gang. The *juru kunci* had more sense than to confront them. He ran all the way back to the village to alert the elders.

"The scoundrel was caught as he tried to sneak back into the village but it was too late to search the forest for the bandits and their stolen treasure. Mbah Merapi had warned the *juru kunci* that he would cleanse the forest of the bandit curse. So if we valued our lives, we should leave immediately in case he had to chase the curse through the village with his mountain fire.

"So that's the truth about the scoundrel, the lost treasure and the Sunda bandits," said Small Aunt, "and why is my tea cup empty?"

"What happened to the scoundrel?" Kancil asked as she filled Small Aunt's cup with the last of the tea.

"He offered himself as a sacrifice to Mbah Merapi and was last seen walking towards the mountain as everybody else was running away. His poor father died of shame," said Small Aunt.

"Did he have any other family?" asked Kitchen Boy. He had a look on his face like he was trying to work out the connections in a puzzle.

Small Aunt looked at him with a wry smile. "We've been better at washing away the past than I thought," she said. "Do you really not know?"

Kitchen Boy shook his head.

"Bibi was his mother and Ida was his sister. She was only a baby at the time, she wouldn't remember him at all. I wonder if she even knows."

Kancil's jaw dropped. Bibi was Ida's *mother*?

11

DISASTER STRIKES

"So you really *are* bandit spawn!" crowed Kitchen Boy as soon as they were on the path back to the village.

"I am *not*," Kancil snapped. "Not everybody from Sunda is a bandit."

"Maybe not, but every bandit is from Sunda."

"That's not true," said Kancil. "I grew up in Sunda and I never met a bandit until I came to Mataram."

"You've met a bandit then?" Kitchen Boy sounded interested.

"Well, not exactly. When we entered the mountains we started travelling at night so we could see their fires and when we slept during the day we had to hide in ditches where we wouldn't be seen. How many bandits have *you* met?"

"A few," he replied vaguely.

"And how did you know they were all from Sunda?" Kancil wasn't going to let him off too easily.

"He talked strangely, a bit like you do, now that I think of it."

"*He* talked strangely? You met one bandit and from that you decide that all bandits must be from Sunda – because *he* talked strangely? It's no wonder everyone on the coast thinks you inlanders are backward!"

"If you meet a bandit in the forest, you don't stop to have a long conversation about where he's from. You just try to appear not worth the effort to rob or kill, and get away as fast as you can. I'm quite good at it. So the point is, I've *seen* plenty of bandits and they all *looked* much the same, and the one I had the misfortune of meeting did talk a bit like you do. I'm sorry, but around here Sunda people have that sort of reputation."

"Well, where *I'm* from, Mataram people don't have *any* sort of reputation because nobody has ever heard of Mataram," Kancil replied.

They walked on in tense silence for a while. Then Kancil remembered something. "You said you'd tell me about the spirits if I told you where I'm from," she said.

"Did I?"

"Yes."

"But you didn't tell me where you were from. I figured it out for myself." Kitchen Boy was wearing his sly smile.

"You don't know the whole story."

"Oh?" Kitchen Boy said.

"My father came from Sunda but his father came from over the sea. Nobody knows where from – Father told me he was a shipwrecked sailor and that he came from a land where there were tigers. *My* father was a trader. He came here when he was young to sell frankincense to the pilgrims when they still used to come to the forest temples. He met my mother and took her back to Sunda where I was born. So I'm from Sunda, from Mataram and from over the sea."

"Interesting," Kitchen Boy said. He was looking at her closely. "I don't suppose your father ever mentioned anything about the tiger stone?"

Kancil shook her head. "What's the tiger stone?"

"Nothing. Forget I mentioned it. Now. A bargain's a bargain. What do you want to know about the spirits?"

Kancil was torn. She wanted to know more about the tiger stone but she didn't quite trust him. Perhaps he had invented the tiger stone to distract her and avoid telling her about the spirits.

"You said that some spirits are made up, like water spirits, to frighten children and keep them safe," she said.

"Yes, and to explain the mysterious disappearance of jewellery," Kitchen Boy added.

"But you said some spirits are real. Have you ever seen a real spirit?"

They had reached the wet season river crossing, where the ravine was narrow enough for a bridge of rough sawn tree trunks to span the gap far above the churning torrent. A thick rope, strung between trees on opposite banks, served as a handrail. Kitchen Boy transferred the *kendi* to his weak arm, holding it close to his chest so he could grasp the rope with his strong arm.

"You don't exactly *see* spirits," he said, "you just know they're there. And you shouldn't mess with them by making up stories about striking a bargain with a spirit to save your mother's life."

"You said you'd seen a spirit with your own eyes. You lied to me!" Kancil grumbled as she stepped off the bridge on the village side of the ravine. She was more annoyed with herself than with Kitchen Boy – she should have known he made that up. Why did she believe him?

"It's not the spirit that you see," said Kitchen Boy. "You see how the animals are behaving. For example, if a gecko bows, it means there's a spirit nearby."

Kancil laughed out loud at this, then quickly covered her mouth. They were in the thick of the forest now, anybody could be listening from the bushes. Kitchen Boy shrugged and they kept walking. He didn't seem to care whether she believed him or not. That bothered her. It wasn't like him not to try to be convincing. Maybe, crazy as it sounded, he was telling the truth. But whoever heard of a gecko bowing?

When they reached the edge of the forest they stopped to rest and drink from the *kendi*. Kancil decided to take another approach. There didn't appear to be anyone nearby. Even so, to be safe she sat close beside him and kept her head down as she murmured, "What about your tiger spirit? The first day I met you, you said your tiger spirit would protect the kitchen and you made a joke about it at the *pondok* before. Were you messing with the spirits then, by making up stories?"

Kitchen Boy looked at her with respect. "Nothing passes *you* by, does it?" he said.

"Tell me the truth," she said, trying to glare at him the way Father used to glare at her. She had never been able to lie in the face of that glare.

"It's true, I do joke about my tiger spirit," said Kitchen Boy, "but that's different. The thing is–" then he stopped. Kancil looked up to see him studying her and chewing his lip, deep in thought. She cocked her head and waited; something told her that Father's glare had worked.

"The thing is, I don't really understand it myself. If you want to know the truth, it scares me. I make a joke of it to make myself less scared.

"I did see a tiger once in the forest, when I was collecting honey. It was the first time they sent me out on my own. I was climbing a tree and the branch gave way. I fell and I must have hit my head because the next thing I remember is waking up on the forest floor with a tiger standing over me. All I could see were her huge golden eyes, and I could feel her paw on my chest, holding me down. I thought I was done for but she just sniffed at my tiger scar then sat back and watched me."

"What did you do?" Kancil breathed.

"I lay still for a while, hoping she'd get bored and go away. That's when I noticed the bowing gecko on a rock next to me."

Kancil looked at him sharply; was he teasing her?

"I know it sounds weird but if you ever see it, you'll know exactly what I mean. Anyway, that was the first time I saw a gecko do that and somehow it scared me more than the tiger did. I stood up, and I ran and ran."

He hit his head, Kancil reminded herself. He could have imagined the whole thing. Somehow, this didn't seem like the time to suggest that. It might break the spell that was revealing a side to Kitchen Boy she hadn't seen before.

"Did you ever see the tiger again?" she asked.

"Maybe," he said slowly. "It was different though. You remember I said I spoke to a bandit once in the forest?"

Kancil nodded.

"Well, I don't really know what happened. He brought out a knife and then … and then there was a noise, something between the sound of thunder and the sound of a tree splitting and the most terrible scream I've ever heard. The next thing I knew I was at this exact spot. I must have run all the way. I couldn't remember any of it. All I remember is the sound and seeing those huge golden eyes right in front of my face."

Kitchen Boy shuddered at the memory then he grinned at Kancil. "So the moral of this story is 'don't mess with Tiger Boy'," he said. The old joking tone had returned to his voice. It didn't irritate Kancil now that she understood why he was doing it.

"That wasn't the first time we met, by the way," he added.

Kancil looked at him, perplexed.

"That day when Ida tried to burn the kitchen down and I said my tiger spirit would protect us, you said it was the day we met. We met the day before, when the prince's messenger came."

Why was he bringing *that* up? wondered Kancil, her cheeks burning at the memory of flailing around in the dirt, trying to hold her *kain* together. Then she remembered the look on his face that day when their eyes first met – the look of recognition.

"Your eyes," he said. "They're not the same as my tiger's eyes but there's something the same about them. It scared me for a moment, I thought maybe ... well, I don't know what I thought. Then I realised you were just an ordinary girl."

Kancil thought of the story her father told about her shipwrecked grandfather's arrival in Sunda. He had won acceptance by coaxing a rogue tiger away from the village into the forest. "They thought he was charmed," Father had said. "He told me there was no magic in it, he just knew how to talk to tigers."

She was about to recount the tale to Kitchen Boy but she stopped herself. Grandfather's story belonged to her and Father. It wasn't for sharing. Instead, she said, "If I were a tiger spirit, you would be the first to get clawed."

"I know. Lucky, eh?" Kitchen Boy laughed. "Come on, it looks like they're having a party down there at the *pondok*. If we hurry, we might get there before they leave. There could be food on offer."

Kancil followed his gaze. Her stomach felt suddenly empty, but it had nothing to do with the prospect of a free snack. It was more like a feeling of dread; that crowd was far too close to her necklace's hiding place for comfort.

As they approached the *pondok*, the feeling intensified. Kancil could see a point where the mud wall of the terraced field above the *pondok* had given way in the rain. Amid the carpet of tender green rice shoots, a muddy line of destruction led straight down to the little shack. Kancil knew what had happened; a river of mud had gushed through the field and under the *pondok*, flushing out whatever lay in the dirt underneath.

The crowd was on the far side of the building. A man with a stick was reaching down to lift something out of the mud. He turned, holding the stick away from his body and the crowd jumped back as though there was a snake coiled around it.

The stick-bearer led a procession back into the village and Kancil and Kitchen Boy joined the tail end. Kitchen Boy was excited, craning his neck, trying to see what the stick-bearer was carrying. Kancil knew exactly what it was. All she could think about was how to stop Mother from finding out that the necklace had been uncovered.

Once through the village gate, the crowd headed straight for Big Uncle's *pendopo*. Someone climbed up to strike the *kentongan* to call the village elders and within minutes the men who spent the evenings lounging in the *pendopo* were gathered together and the crowd had increased fourfold.

A bowl of water was fetched and the muddy necklace dropped into it. Bapak Iya, the village elder who always agreed with Big Uncle, prodded the necklace to loosen the mud from the shells. The corners of his mouth were turned down in distaste, as though he were poking at a very smelly dead animal.

Why can't they just throw it away and get on with their lives? Kancil wondered. I know nothing much happens in this place, but this is ridiculous!

Bapak Iya lifted the necklace up and there was a hush as everybody gazed at the string of tiny cowry shells now glistening in the sunlight.

"Are they …?" Bapak Iya asked, his voice trailing off as he turned to Big Uncle.

Big Uncle was nodding, a grim look on his face. "*Sea*shells," he said.

Kancil could see Bibi and Ida standing near the courtyard gate. Ida was relaying messages to the pavilion where Big Aunt and Citra sat. Kancil couldn't see Mother but that gave her little comfort; perhaps she was so ill that she couldn't leave her bed. Kancil had to find her to make sure she was all right.

The crowd was so thick that Kancil was forced to squeeze through to reach the courtyard gate. "It must be a curse," she heard Bapak Iya say, "a curse from the sea to stop our mountain lands from prospering under the protection of the prince." His voice rose an octave. "A *bandit* curse!"

Kancil stumbled into the open at the very moment Bapak Iya squeaked out this last statement, his finger pointing at the offending item that hung from the muddy stick. He looked such a fool, his eyes fixed in terror on the pretty shells that Father had strung together that last evening on the beach.

How Father would laugh if he could see this, Kancil thought.

As she turned to slip through the courtyard gate, she caught sight of Kitchen Boy standing at the edge of the crowd. He was looking over her shoulder. Kancil turned to see what he was looking at. Bibi was standing at the gate, a look of triumph in her eyes. Kancil remembered how upset Mother had been in the *pondok* when she saw the necklace. She understood why now.

"Her!" Bibi shrieked, a glob of spittle flying from her mouth. She raised her walking cane and poked Kancil in the chest. "It's her, I knew it! She's bandit spawn, you can see it in her thieving eyes. We should never have let her and her good-for-nothing mother into the village!"

Kancil understood why Bibi had it in for her and Mother now that she had heard Small Aunt's story. However, understanding didn't lessen the pain in her chest as Bibi poked at her again and again, pushing her backwards until she was wedged between the cane and the edge of the *pendopo*.

The crowd fell silent. Kancil could hear someone moving towards her across the *pendopo* floor. She held her breath and braced herself, expecting to be grabbed around the neck and dragged into the *pendopo* for questioning. Instead, Big Uncle's hand reached over her head and took hold of Bibi's cane. With a quick jab he set Bibi off balance. She staggered backwards and the cane clattered to the ground.

"My niece," Big Uncle's voice boomed from the *pendopo*, "is *not* bandit spawn and you, old woman, will remember your place in my household!"

Bibi's face turned a colour that Kancil had never seen on a face before. It was a shade of purple much better suited to a ripe mangosteen than to anything that breathed. With that thought, Kancil remembered to breathe again. With her breath, her senses returned and she ran through the gate. Behind her, she could hear Big Uncle proclaiming to the crowd: "This worthless charm shall be ground to dust and strewn in the river to be carried far away from here. Whoever planted this curse has failed, and that is all there is to be said on the matter. Now bring me a grinding stone!"

It's for the best, Kancil told herself as she ran down the narrow passageway to the rickety shack. It didn't help. Her last connection to her father was being destroyed.

12

A VISION

"They found the necklace, didn't they?" Mother asked. She seemed to have shrunk since this morning and her face was deathly pale.

Kancil pursed her lips and gave Mother a warning look. She didn't think Bibi was anywhere nearby but she wasn't going to take any chances. If Bibi hated her before, she must hate her tenfold now. She would be looking for any opportunity to prove that she was right about Kancil being a bandit's child.

Kancil untied the basket from her back and emptied its contents onto the sleeping platform. Parcels wrapped in banana leaves scattered across the mat. She didn't know which one was the *jamu* for Mother.

Where is Kitchen Boy? she wondered. It was typical of him to be somewhere else when she needed him.

At that very moment she saw him striding down the passageway with Bibi and Ida following in his wake.

"Why is the *jamu* scattered all over this dirty floor?" Bibi demanded as she approached, her cane thumping on the ground. "You've stolen some, haven't you, you thieving bint?"

Kancil drew her legs under her, folded her hands in her lap and bowed her head – she had learned this was the best position to defend herself against Bibi's cane.

"Now, now, Bibi, don't excite yourself," said Kitchen Boy. "I told her to get the *jamu* out in the fresh air as soon as we got here."

He reached out for one of the packages. "So," he cleared his throat as though preparing to give a long speech. Then he gave Bibi a detailed explanation of how to prepare each *jamu* for Citra. He added several embellishments to the instructions Small Aunt had given him to make the process seem more complicated.

Kancil willed him to hear Mother's shallow breathing – why was he wasting time teasing Bibi? He looked up at Bibi in the middle of a particularly complicated instruction. "Perhaps it would be better if I prepared the *jamu* for you? I really don't mind," he said sweetly.

"Why would you offer? What's in it for you?" Bibi asked, eyeing him suspiciously.

"Well …" he said, "I can tell you're going to ask me

to repeat each instruction at least ten times so I think it might be easier if I prepare the *jamu* myself. I can do it right here so I'm out of your way and the girl can help me. She might as well make herself useful."

"There's sickness here," said Bibi, curling her lip at Mother. "This is no place to prepare *jamu* for a princess!"

"Let's not get ahead of ourselves," said Kitchen Boy with a grin. Then he shook his head. "We couldn't possibly prepare this *jamu* in the kitchen, it's far too potent to be mixed in that confined space. No, here will do nicely. Ida, would you get the medicine grinding stone and a brazier for me? I'll need fresh water too, and gourds." He turned his back on Bibi, who walked away meekly, leaving Kancil to wonder how Kitchen Boy managed to exert such power over them all.

Once Bibi and Ida were out of the way, Kitchen Boy didn't waste any time. He instructed Kancil to grind the dry ingredients for Mother's tonic while he extracted the juices from the wet ingredients. Mother tried to raise herself to help, but he shooed her back to bed and unrolled a small dark stick of something gummy from the waist of his *sarung*. "Your sister sends her greetings and says you should do everything I tell you. The first thing you have to do is chew on this." He thrust the gum stick into her hand.

Mother gave Kancil a questioning look and Kancil nodded encouragingly.

"It's safe to talk," said Kitchen Boy. "They've gone out the front."

Mother turned to Kancil. "He knows?" she groaned.

Kitchen Boy looked from Kancil to Mother. Then he shrugged and returned to straining the juice into the water that was bubbling over the brazier. "Never mind. It's only me who knows, the rest of them are far too stupid. What's the story with those shells, by the way?"

Kancil shook her head firmly. Mother lay back down, exhausted. "No fun at all, you two," said Kitchen Boy.

When Mother's *jamu* tonic was prepared and cooling, Kancil moved on to mixing Citra's beauty preparations, most of which she could do without direction from Kitchen Boy – Small Aunt's instructions had been quite straightforward. Meanwhile, Kitchen Boy was huddled intently over a bundle of dried herbs and strips of curling tree bark. He carefully divided these ingredients into five small piles that he lined up on separate banana leaves beside the brazier. He poked at the coals to reduce the heat without killing the fire.

"It's time," he said to Kancil, motioning towards the tonic they had prepared for Mother. "She should drink half now and half in the morning. I'll go down the passageway to keep watch – if anyone sees her drinking this, they'll think she's stealing Citra's *jamu*. If you hear this sound," he made a noise through his teeth that sounded almost like the rustle of bamboo in a breeze, "put it away and get back to grinding Citra's *jamu*."

Kancil helped Mother to sit up properly. Her ears were tuned to the slightest sound and she almost spilled the *jamu*, she was so jumpy. Mother took such tiny sips that Kancil wondered if she might still be drinking the first half when morning came. Then she heard the rustle of bamboo. She surprised herself at how calmly she helped Mother lie back and returned to her proper post, even though her heart was racing. As it was, Kitchen Boy had given her plenty of warning and she was energetically grinding Citra's *jamu* ingredients when the chickens next door started clucking.

Ida stomped past on her way to the kitchen for the men's drinks. "Where's the boy?" she called out as she passed. Kancil shrugged, wondering how he had managed to hide himself so well that Ida hadn't met him in the passageway.

Returning to her grinding stone, Kancil tried to steer her thoughts to a safe topic but they kept leaping back to what Mother had said last night about her having a home here when she was gone. Even if Small Aunt's *jamu* saved her from this illness, Kancil had to accept that one day she would be alone unless her brother, Agus, miraculously reappeared.

That would depend on him still being alive, free and knowing where to find her. No, that was a few too many miracles. She had found out who the scoundrel was and his connection to the temple treasures. Her father's spirit had led her to that discovery, she was sure of that now. Yet she couldn't fathom how that knowledge would help to find her brother and when she tried to summon Father's voice to guide her, she heard only the grinding sound of her shell necklace being crushed.

Big Uncle had shown today that he would protect her – or was he protecting his family's reputation? Despite Mother's assurances, Kancil didn't believe she could trust him. In any case, he was older than Mother, and Kancil had no illusions that either Big Aunt or Citra would feel obliged to treat her like a proper member of the family if Big Uncle wasn't there to speak on her behalf. That was the problem, she told herself. So long as she had to rely on others to speak for her, she was stuck.

Kitchen Boy had proven to be a surprise ally and Small Aunt, for all her sharp words, seemed to be warming to her, but in her heart Kancil knew that she had to get her voice back. The only way she could see herself doing that was by leaving the village. But where could she go and how could she get there?

Suddenly, Kitchen Boy was beside her, peering over her shoulder at the grinding stone. "You're working too fast," he said. "If you finish the grinding, Bibi will decide you've finished everything and send Ida to collect the brazier. We need the brazier for your Mother's *jamu*."

Kancil nodded and slowed her pace to a gentle rocking motion. She didn't mind being told she was working too hard.

Kitchen Boy placed the first bundle of *jamu* ingredients over the coals. "Ibu Sumirah," he said, turning to Mother, "do you think you could lie down over here where I can direct the smoke? You should try to sleep and let the *jamu* do its work."

"I think I've forgotten how to sleep," said Mother.

Kancil had an idea. "Tell us a story," she whispered to Kitchen Boy.

"What?" he asked.

"Tell us a story," she repeated. "It might help Mother to sleep and it will stop me thinking."

"Thinking what?"

"Just thinking. Stop asking questions and tell us a story."

Kitchen Boy frowned. Kancil gave him an exasperated look. This was not the moment for the born storyteller to be lost for words.

"All right," said Kitchen Boy, finally. "Let me get this

going first." He was gently fanning the coals with a square of woven palm leaf to encourage the *jamu* to smoke. Once a thin ribbon of smoke started to rise from the carefully arranged pile, he turned his wrist so that the fan directed the smoke over Mother's nose. Kancil had never seen *jamu* used in this way. Small Aunt, she decided, was no ordinary *jamu* maker.

She sniffed at the air. The fragrance of the *jamu* was so delicate that it barely registered over the more pungent aromas of the ingredients she was grinding for Citra.

"One day I was out collecting honey near the forest temples and it started to rain," Kitchen Boy began. "I took shelter in the tallest temple and discovered someone was already there. Luckily for me he was a holy man, not a bandit, and while we waited for the rain to stop, I gave him some of my honey and he told me a story about how the temples were built.

"It all began with a prince. I forget his name now; let's call him Bhre Mataram. And there was a princess, let's call our princess Raden Ajeng Citra. It will help us get used to thinking of Citra as a princess.

"Anyway, Bhre Mataram decided that Raden Ajeng Citra would be his bride, but she had other ideas. You can't just tell a prince that you won't marry him though, so Raden Ajeng Citra had to come up with a face-saving way of refusing him. For some reason, she decided to set him a challenge. He was to build her one thousand temples in one night and if he succeeded, she would marry him."

The first pile of *jamu* was spent and Kitchen Boy paused while he set the next pile on the brazier. Kancil leaned over her grinding stone to look at Mother; her chest was rising and falling rhythmically and her eyes were closed. She was asleep.

Kitchen Boy looked pleased. He sat back on his heels while he continued to fan the smoke across Mother's face.

Kancil prodded him with her foot. "Finish the story," she signed to him.

When Kancil woke the next morning, Mother was still sleeping peacefully and a faint sweet and smoky smell hung about the shack. Kancil tried to ease herself carefully off the sleeping platform so as not to wake her mother but that was impossible. Mother sat up with a gasp and looked around her in confusion.

"Are you well?" Kancil signed.

Mother's forehead was creased with the effort of remembering something; it was replaced with a look of horror as the memory came back to her.

"Child!" she breathed. "The prince – he's going to turn Citra to stone. I've seen it in a vision!"

Kancil stared. Mother looked much healthier than she had for weeks, but had she gone mad?"

"I must go and warn my brother," Mother said, standing up.

Kancil grabbed her and pulled her back to the sleeping mat. "Remember," she signed, "the story, it was the story about the princess." This was too hard to sign but she didn't dare speak – the chickens next door were restless and Kancil wouldn't be surprised if Bibi was spying on them. She looked around, just in time to see Kitchen Boy returning from his early morning errands. She motioned urgently to him to join them.

"Tell him," she signed to Mother when he arrived.

"Kancil, your friend is very clever, but he's only a boy. Now let me go, I must warn my brother. There's not a moment to lose."

Kancil clutched at Mother's wrist. She couldn't let her tell the story to Big Uncle – he would think that Mother was possessed and lock her up. Kancil herself would have thought she was possessed if not for that sweet smell in the air. Could last night's *jamu* be responsible? She had had some strange dreams about temples and princesses herself. She had no doubt they were dreams, not visions, but she hadn't been in the direct line of the smoke.

"Are you well, Ibu?" Kitchen Boy asked.

"Quite well, thank you, and I promise I will drink

the rest of the *jamu* presently. First, I must warn my brother. I have had the most terrible vision that the prince will turn Citra to stone."

Kitchen Boy looked at Kancil quizzically. "Remind her!" Kancil signed to him. What was in that smoke? she wondered.

"That's … interesting …" Kitchen Boy was looking at Mother now. "Are you sure, Ibu, that you are not confusing Citra and the prince with the story I told last night? You remember the story, don't you?"

Mother looked uncertain and Kancil nudged Kitchen Boy. "*Remind* her!" she signed to him again.

"It was the story the holy man told me about how the temples were built. The prince turned the princess to stone after she tried to trick him." Kitchen Boy paused, looking for some sign of recognition in Mother's face. She wasn't trying to leave the shack now but she didn't look convinced.

"Remember," he continued gently, "the princess challenged him to build one thousand temples in one night. She wasn't expecting him to enlist the help of demons to complete the task. When it looked like he might succeed, she cheated. She got all the villagers to light their fires and rattle their pots and pans so the roosters would think it was dawn. The prince and his demons had built nine hundred and ninety-nine temples. When he heard the roosters crowing, he gave up. When the real sun rose, he realised he'd been tricked so he had his demons turn the princess to stone and she became the thousandth temple."

A look of realisation had spread over Mother's face as Kitchen Boy spoke and now she put her hand to her mouth. "Of course," she said. "How strange, I was so sure when I woke up that it was a vision of Citra's future. It wasn't until I heard your voice just now that I remembered you telling me. Oh, you must think I'm a fool!"

"Not at all, Ibu," Kitchen Boy reassured her. "You may well be right. The prince will most probably *think* about turning Citra to stone once he discovers how annoying she is, but I don't think it's so easy to find the necessary demons to do the job these days."

13

THE *DALANG*

Mother drank her morning *jamu* and Kitchen Boy gave Kancil two lidded baskets, each one lined with banana leaf and filled with raw *jamu* ingredients.

"This one is to make more tonic if she needs it," he told Kancil. "You'll have to get hold of the grinding stone again to prepare it. Once it's ground it will only last a day or two at the most.

"These are the smoking ingredients," he continued, opening the other basket to reveal the dried herbs and bark that he had smoked on the brazier the night before. "You shouldn't need them again, but keep them just in case."

"Are you crazy?" Kancil signed to him. "We should destroy these!"

"Why?" Kitchen Boy asked, looking puzzled.

"Because they caused …" she couldn't think of a way to sign what had happened to Mother, but she could tell from Kitchen Boy's face that he knew what she was trying to say.

"Do you think the *jamu* caused that?" he asked.

Kancil rolled her eyes; surely he had figured that out for himself.

"You're quite smart really, aren't you?" Kitchen Boy said. "You might be right about the *jamu* causing the dream. You're wrong about destroying it, though. Your aunt went to a lot of trouble to gather those ingredients. They're not the ordinary beauty muck she sent for Citra. We'd better keep these in the kitchen where they'll be safe from weather and insects."

"Under here," he said as he crawled under a shelf in the darkest corner of the kitchen. He shifted a folded mat out of the way and lifted the heavy lid from a large clay jar, dropping the baskets inside.

"Don't worry," he said, "nobody uses this jar except me."

Kancil turned away to tend the fire.

"Why are you in such a bad mood?" Kitchen Boy asked.

Kancil pointed her chin towards the jar and shook her head, turning the corners of her mouth down.

"Bah," muttered Kitchen Boy. "Some people are never satisfied! The *jamu* cured her, didn't it? And double-quick time too. Besides, there was no harm done, was there? I, for one, quite liked her vision."

Kancil looked around for something to throw at him. She stopped herself – that was the sort of thing Bibi would do. She gave him a scathing look instead and picked up the broom.

"Maybe you're jealous that it's Citra marrying the prince, not you."

Kancil laughed soundlessly and began working the broom from the back corner towards the kitchen door. She was surprised to see Kitchen Boy pick up the bucket and sprinkle water on the floor to settle the dust. What a strange day she was having! First, her seriously ill mother woke up cured (if she was prepared to accept Kitchen Boy's assurance that crazy visions didn't count for anything), and now Kitchen Boy was helping her with her chores. A smile spread across her face; she was actually happy!

Then Kancil heard the sound of Bibi's cane thumping down the path. It sounded angrier than usual, if that were possible. Kancil exchanged a glance with Kitchen Boy and he pulled a face. "Just when I thought I was going to have a good day," he whispered. They grinned at each other.

"Why isn't the rice cooking?" Bibi demanded, sniffing

at the air as she stomped in. Then the tray of rice that Kitchen Boy had left on the hulling bench caught her eye. "Why is the rice not even *hulled* yet?" she bellowed. "What have you been doing all morning, you lazy bint?" She picked up the nearest thing to hand and threw it at Kancil's head. Kancil ducked as the coconut shell flew past. She need not have bothered – Bibi's aim was way off today. Usually, that was a sign that something was really bothering her.

"You, boy," Bibi said. "Go and get two more measures of rice. And you, bint! You'd better get hulling that rice faster than ever before or your life won't be worth living."

Kancil stowed her broom and went to the long hulling bench, wondering if "bint" was an improvement on "bandit spawn". She decided to assume that it was. She scooped some of the rice from the tray into one of the two hollowed-out bowls in the bench. As she lifted the pounding rod into position, Ida tried to walk past. Bibi blocked her way.

"There's a reason there are two holes in that thing," Bibi said, nodding towards the hulling bench.

"That's *her* job!" whined Ida, glaring at Kancil.

"And today it's your job too," said Bibi. "A *dalang* and his troupe are expected to arrive at any moment and I have to feed them – as if I didn't have enough to do already."

Kancil had heard the men discussing the *dalang*, the puppet master, in the *pendopo* a week previously. Dalang Mulyo was from the port of Pekalongan. He travelled around the kingdom with his *wayang* puppets and *gamelan* musicians, performing at weddings and ceremonies in villages that didn't have their own *dalang*.

Kitchen Boy could barely contain his excitement when he heard that the *dalang* and his troupe had arrived and were resting in the *pendopo* at the north gate. "I'll take the refreshments to them," he offered, reaching for the tray of sticky rice cakes that Bibi had prepared.

"The girl can go," Bibi ordered.

Seeing Kitchen Boy's crestfallen face, Kancil did her best to look wobbly when she lifted the tray onto her head and tried to pick up the water *kendi*.

"Bah!" fumed Bibi. "You useless wretch! Boy, take the *kendi* from her before she drops it. Get out of here the pair of you!"

When Kancil and Kitchen Boy arrived with the refreshments, they found that a swarm of children had already formed around the perimeter of the north gate *pendopo*.

Inside the *pendopo*, a group of weary travellers lounged against a jumble of boxes and baskets. A woman, who

Kancil figured must be the *pesinden* singer, was sitting on the far edge of the *pendopo*, looking bored and fanning herself with a delicate sandalwood fan. Four men were positioned around the belongings. Two appeared to be asleep while the other two were observing the throng of children with amusement.

In the middle of the *pendopo* was a man with white hair, who must be the *dalang*. His eyes were closed but a small smile played on his lips as he listened to the children's whispers. His hand was resting gently on the lid of a long wooden box.

"Please, Bapak Dalang, won't you show us your puppets?" asked one brave child after much prodding from his companions.

Dalang Mulyo opened one eye and fixed it on the little boy. "Oh, I couldn't possibly do that," he said.

"Can't we have a quick look?" the boy persisted.

The *dalang* shook his head sadly. "They've had such an arduous journey and they need their rest. You'll have to wait until they are ready to perform."

The village children looked at each other and giggled.

"But I've never *seen* a shadow puppet," the boy made one final appeal.

"What *is* that child going on about? I can't understand a word these inland children say," the singer said to nobody in particular. She spoke the Jawa language but her coastal dialect was quite different to the inland dialect of the village. She sounded almost like she was speaking the Sunda language.

Kancil looked around to see if Kitchen Boy or the children had noticed, but they were focussing intently on the *dalang* and the wooden box. For a moment Kancil felt annoyed; it wasn't fair that a travelling singer could get away with sounding like she came from Sunda while Kancil had to pretend to be mute to hide her origins.

Then an idea popped into her head. Perhaps the *dalang*'s troupe could be her means of escape from the village. If she could make herself useful to them in some way, they might take her with them when they returned to Pekalongan.

That was the port where she and Mother had ended their sea journey in the clove trader's boat and begun their long journey inland. It must be somewhere between Sunda and that awful place, Bubat. If Agus had survived the massacre and escaped imprisonment, he would probably have passed through Pekalongan on his way back home. She might find a trace of him there.

The puzzle in her dream – the scoundrel, the temple treasures, Agus – would have to remain unsolved. That's all right, she told herself, I'm using the sense that

Mother taught me in the market – watch and listen and make the most of opportunities. It might not be as comforting as having Father's spirit to guide me, but it could prove more reliable.

14

PREPARATIONS

The next morning, every task was at least doubled. Kitchen Boy dumped a sack of rice on the hulling bench and left immediately to look for firewood. Ida grumbled as she hauled a huge pile of washing onto her back, leaving Kancil to hull the rice by herself.

Throughout the morning the sound of *gamelan* music, rising and falling in intensity, could be heard coming from the north *pendopo*. The *pendopo* in front of Big Uncle's house, usually so quiet during the day, was alive with the chatter of girls and young women gathered to make decorations for the welcome ceremony.

Two of Big Uncle's pigs had been slaughtered for the ceremony and Bapak Pohon, the giant, spent the morning under the tamarind tree expertly preparing the carcasses. Kancil laughed now at how he had frightened her the first time she met him. Nowadays, he made a special point of greeting her whenever he visited to collect supplies for the *joglo* or to perform his role as village butcher. What was more, Bibi was less severe when he was there to witness her cruelty.

"The scout's back," said Kitchen Boy as he burst through the door with a load of firewood. "He spotted the prince at the high spring. He'll definitely be here by nightfall."

"What did he look like?" asked Ida. It was the first time Kancil had heard her sound excited about anything.

Kitchen Boy shrugged. "The scout only got close enough to see where he was and came straight back," he said.

"Well, what *did* he see?" demanded Bibi. Nothing in the world could make her sound excited.

"He saw a *jempana* carriage carried by six bearers. He couldn't see into the *jempana* because the parasol bearer kept getting in the way. He was sure it must be the prince, though, because the *jempana* and the parasol were very grand."

"And that's all?" Bapak Pohon bellowed in mock amazement. "A prince and seven bearers? No kitchen staff, no livestock? I hope he's not planning to stay too long or we'll have no food to feed ourselves when he's gone."

Mother could rest now she had made new *kain* and *kemben* for Big Aunt and Citra and finished all the cloths for the prince's *joglo*. She was in the sleeping shack, patching a well-worn *kain* when Kancil arrived for the midday rest.

"This is for you to wear tonight at the prince's welcome," Mother said, holding up the *kain* as Kancil climbed onto the bamboo platform. "It's a gift from your cousin."

Kancil handed her the small parcel of rice that was her midday meal. The chickens in the shack next door were quiet so she knew it was safe to talk. "Be careful," she said, "there will probably be stones in the rice. I didn't have time to pick over it properly before I cooked it."

She glanced at the *kain*. "Is that the one she threw out when you gave her the new one you made?" she asked. Mother pursed her lips and Kancil knew that she must feel bad about something – Kancil wouldn't normally get away with an ungrateful comment without a rebuke at the very least.

Mother folded the *kain* and unwrapped her rice. She cleared her throat as if she were about to say something. Then she seemed to change her mind. They sat in silence for a while, chewing the bland rice and occasionally picking out a small stone and flicking it onto the path. Kancil could feel the tension of her mother's unspoken words.

"I know I'm not to sit with the family at the welcome ceremony," she said. "Bibi told me." Bibi had, in fact, taken particular glee in conveying that message from Big Aunt to Kancil.

Mother looked apologetic.

"It's all right," Kancil said with a shrug. "I wouldn't want to sit near Citra anyway."

"Child, really! You shouldn't say such things," Mother replied. Her voice was so tired and weak that the rebuke had little impact. Mother was alive, and for that Kancil was grateful, yet there was something missing; the determination that had kept her strong all the way from the coast to the village had been worn away, leaving nothing but gratitude to her horrible family for *allowing* her to survive.

After the midday rest, Kancil was sent to the *pendopo* at the front of the house to help with preparations for the welcome ceremony. Girls and young women were sitting in circles around piles of banana leaves, palm fronds and flowers. Everybody's hands were busy with something: splicing palm fronds to weave offering baskets, fashioning banana leaves into hanging decorations or plaiting jasmine and cempaka flowers to make dancers' headdresses.

Kancil stood on the step, hesitating; the groups all looked complete. Wherever she sat she would be pushing in. She realised that she had become so used to being invisible that the thought of drawing attention to herself made her skin prickle.

Then another thought came to her. Was she becoming like Mother? Afraid to make a scene and accepting the scraps her family threw her? She would rather be like Kitchen Boy. He was an outcast but he didn't let it bother him. In fact, he made the most of the freedom that his status afforded him. Or Small Aunt – she didn't try to fit in and she didn't appear to suffer for it. Of course, both Kitchen Boy and Small Aunt had skills the village needed: Small Aunt knew powerful *jamu* remedies and Kitchen Boy knew where to find wild honey and pepper. Kancil couldn't think of any skill she had that made her indispensable to the village – or to the *dalang*'s troupe, for that matter.

Well, she thought, at least I know how to weave a temple basket. I'm not completely useless.

She sat down next to Hen, one of the girls from the washing pool, and set to work. She soon relaxed into the rhythm of attaching palm fronds to a circle of cane then folding and overlapping them to make a basket as she listened to her companions speculate about what the prince would look like and whether he would approve of the festivities they had planned for him.

Citra was sitting nearby with a group of well-dressed girls, plaiting flowers into dancers' headdresses for the welcome dance. In contrast to the washing girls, their conversation seemed forced, as though the girls weren't sure how they should behave in the company of someone about to become a prince's consort.

Kancil had almost finished her basket when Citra's voice broke through the cheerful buzz in the *pendopo*. "We'll never get these done in time!" she whined. "Here, you can help," she reached over and dumped a tray of flowers and twine in front of Kancil.

A gentle breeze played around the *pendopo*, carrying the flowers' perfume to her nostrils. It's better than straining coconut oil, she told herself as she began threading the flowers through the twine.

"Now, girls, where are my dancers? The prince will be here by nightfall, we must practise!" Ibu Tari was standing on the *pendopo* steps, her eyes shining with excitement. "And what about the headdresses? Are they ready?" she added.

"Here are mine, Ibu," Citra leaped up, grabbing Kancil's headdresses. Kancil could only watch in disbelief as her cousin held out the delicate chains to the old woman while Citra's own lumpy efforts lay in a forlorn pile where she had been sitting.

"Oh, they're beautiful, well done," beamed Ibu Tari. As she spoke, Big Aunt and Mother emerged from the courtyard dressed in their temple clothes. "Look at the work Citra has done," Ibu Tari said, showing them the flower chains.

Big Aunt looked at the flowers. She didn't say anything.

"Well done, dear," said Mother, filling the awkward silence. Kancil glared at her but she wasn't looking, she had stepped back behind Big Aunt, her head bowed.

Something caught Big Aunt's eye and she reached out for one of the chains. "This one's coming apart," she said, holding the end of the chain before Citra's eyes. "You really should be more thorough."

Kancil didn't know whether to be cross with herself for forgetting to tie off the plait or pleased for getting her cousin into trouble. "Good *work*!" murmured Hen. Kancil settled on being pleased.

Two temple baskets filled with fruit, cakes and flowers were sitting on the edge of the *pendopo*. Mother helped Big Aunt lift one onto her head then she took the other for herself and they both left for the temple. The dancers, who turned out to be almost all of the girls in the *pendopo*, followed Ibu Tari to practise, leaving only a few girls to gather together the decorations and fill the remaining temple baskets for the other village women to carry.

Bibi and Ida emerged from the courtyard dressed for the temple just as Kancil was putting away the broom after sweeping all the leftover palm fronds and flowers into the bushes.

"Make sure you sweep the courtyard too before you're done," Bibi called out as they passed.

15

THE PRINCE

Kancil was hurrying along the main path that led to the north *pendopo* when a low whistle stopped her in her tracks. She listened and there it was again, coming from somewhere along a narrow path that branched off from the main way.

Trees towered over both sides of the path, their branches meeting in a tangle overhead, blocking out all but the most persistent shards of afternoon light. Kancil stepped cautiously towards the sound, peering into the gloom. She leaped back as a figure dropped from an overhanging branch. It was Kitchen Boy. She pretended to throw a stone at him and he ducked then laughed.

"What took you so long?" he asked. Kancil mimed sweeping.

"Ah, you're good," he said. "Come on then." With

that he turned and started walking down the dark path.

Kancil stayed where she was and waited for him to stop messing around. He kept walking. She clapped her hands to get his attention and he turned.

Kancil pointed at Kitchen Boy and shrugged her shoulders to make a question.

"Who am I?" Kitchen Boy asked, a mock puzzled look on his face. "You know who I am. Have you had a knock on the head?"

Kancil glared at him. He was being stupid on purpose. She pointed at him again then walked two fingers across the palm of her other hand and shrugged her shoulders. She exaggerated her movements the way people exaggerated their speech when they spoke to her.

"Where am I going? I'm going to the north *pendopo*, of course."

Kancil pointed back towards the main path. A few stragglers were still making their way along it, their steps hurried. She turned to follow them.

"I wouldn't go that way if I were you," Kitchen Boy said. "At best you'll spend the evening with your nose squashed into somebody's back. It's more likely one of the cooks will put you to work over the cooking fire behind the temple where you won't get to see anything."

He continued down the path. Kancil followed him. She didn't like the way the path turned into a dark tunnel through the trees but she certainly didn't want to spend the evening bent over a charcoal fire, roasting food for other people to eat.

Kitchen Boy bounded ahead and Kancil struggled to keep him in sight in the fading light. She could hear the *gamelan* music not far away so the path must be skirting around the back of the north *pendopo*. Suddenly, the path stopped at a dead end in front of a high bamboo fence. Kitchen Boy was nowhere to be seen.

The low whistle came again, this time from directly above Kancil's head. She looked up and there was Kitchen Boy grinning down at her from the branch of a huge rambutan tree.

"Walk that way ten paces," he called in a hoarse whisper, "and you'll find the trunk."

Kancil followed his directions. The tree trunk was broad and smooth and offered no obvious foothold for climbing. At home on the coast, coconut trees grew at angles to the ground, leaning out to sea. You could walk up them without even holding on. This tree was a totally different prospect.

Why, oh why, did she follow Kitchen Boy? Now she would have to run all the way back down that horrible dark path by herself. She kicked at the tree.

"Hurry up!" Kitchen Boy had returned a little way down the branch. "Put your foot there," he pointed to a slight bulge in the trunk at knee height, "then leap up and put your other foot there," he pointed to a fork in the trunk near Kancil's head. "After that, it's easy."

Kancil took a deep breath. Climbing the tree looked like an impossible feat but if she gave up now, she would never hear the end of it from Kitchen Boy and he would be right – if he could climb it with his arm as it was, what excuse did she have?

She hitched up her *kain* and checked that her *kemben* was secure. She had a sudden flashback to the day she arrived in the village, scrabbling around in the dirt, trying to hold her clothing together while Kitchen Boy laughed.

Well, she thought grimly, I'll either die of embarrassment or a knock to the head when I fall out of this ridiculous tree. Either way, I won't have to suffer another day in Bibi's kitchen.

Before she had time for second thoughts, Kancil gripped the trunk with one foot and levered herself up. Her other foot didn't quite reached the fork. Desperately, she lunged forwards, reaching with her arms for the trunk.

Miraculously, her knee caught in the fork as her body started to scrape down the tree trunk. The pain brought stars to her eyes, but she had enough grip to pitch herself forwards and grab at the bark with her fingers.

With all her might, Kancil dragged herself up into the tree. She was surprised at how strong her arms were – perhaps the hours spent slaving in Bibi's kitchen hadn't been for nothing after all. She managed to get her other foot into the fork and push herself up to a standing position. She clung to a branch, her body shaking all over.

"Not exceptionally graceful, but not a bad effort all the same," Kitchen Boy called softly from above.

"I can't believe I risked death just to get a better view of a Majapahit prince!" Kancil whispered back, her voice was as shaky as her body.

"Put your foot there and grab that branch," Kitchen Boy instructed.

"Follow me to that fork. You'll get a much better view." He pointed to a further branch that looked to Kancil to be much too flimsy to hold them both, but curiosity got the better of her fear.

The branch was stronger than it looked and Kitchen Boy was right, they had a much better view – not only could they see over the roof of the *pendopo* to the open space in front of the temple gate, they could also see behind them, over the high bamboo fence.

Kancil twisted to look down into the garden behind the fence. Near the fence it was an overgrown mass of frangipani and hibiscus. Further back, she could make out the shape of a timber house, almost hidden behind unkempt fruit trees. A movement caught her eye – three figures were making their way carefully through the tangled undergrowth towards the *pendopo*. As they drew closer, Kancil realised it was Dalang Mulyo, the *pesinden* singer and one of the musicians.

She nudged Kitchen Boy. "Whose house is that?" she asked.

"That," Kitchen Boy said dramatically, "is the house where the scoundrel was born."

"Really?" Kancil breathed.

"I only made the connection myself when we visited Ibu Jamu the other day."

"It looks … haunted."

Kitchen Boy nodded. "They say when the mountain, Mbah Merapi, wreaked vengeance on the village all those years ago, the only buildings left standing were the stone shrines in the temple and that house. Even the garden survived, although everything was covered in ash so it looked as if it had all turned to stone."

"How would that make it haunted? I'd have thought it would make it lucky."

"Except that when everybody ran away from Mbah Merapi, the scoundrel's father stayed and he was still there when they returned, sitting in front of the family shrine as though he was meditating. He had turned to stone like the rest of the garden.

"When the rain came, it washed away the ash from

all the plants. They recovered so quickly that you could see the new buds growing before your eyes. But when the rain fell on the man, it didn't bring him back to life. He melted away in a river of silt."

"Really?" Kancil said again. Then she looked at him sharply. "How do you know? You weren't there."

"Everybody knows the story of the haunted house," said Kitchen Boy. "It's just the connection with the scoundrel that the old people fail to mention.

"Anyway, after the rain, nobody could bear to watch the garden growing. There was something wrong about it. So the first thing they did, even before they rebuilt their own homes, was to build that high fence. Not long after, the night watchmen started hearing noises inside. Nobody was game to go in."

"It doesn't seem very hospitable to put up the *dalang* and his family in a haunted house," Kancil said.

"Maybe not, but *dalangs* are different to ordinary people. Bapak Pohon told me a *dalang* meditates before a performance so the gods will breathe life into his puppets. If you were doing that sort of thing regularly, you'd have to get used to the company of the not exactly living and breathing."

"I guess you're right," said Kancil. A shiver ran down her spine when she looked into the garden. If she managed to escape from the village with the *dalang*'s troupe, she was going to have to live like them, and if her plan to find Agus didn't work out, she might be living like them for a very long time. Did she want to spend the rest of her days moving from haunted house to haunted house?

Kitchen Boy nodded towards the roof of the *pendopo* below them. It blocked their view of the musicians inside, tapping their small hammers on the tuned metal rods of the *gamelan* instruments.

"Tomorrow, for the *wayang* puppet performance, we need to be under that roof so we can see the puppets," he said. "I got us up here tonight so I think it's only fair that you get us in there tomorrow. I suggest you work your charm on the singer. She's been on the road for a long time without a servant. If you were to offer her a nice cup of tea, she'd be completely in your power."

Kancil nodded. She was only half-listening. The village elders and their families were moving to their seats in front of the crowd. Big Uncle led the way, seating himself with a flourish on a teak bench that raised him a little above the people around him. Big Aunt kneeled on a mat beside him and Mother kneeled behind them both, leaving a space beside Big Aunt for Citra who would, of course, be leading the welcome dance. Kancil hoped Citra was as bad at dancing as she was at making dancers' headdresses.

"There he is!" Kitchen Boy pointed towards a black and white parasol that had just emerged from the forest and was bobbing down the path through the terraced fields. The lookout saw the parasol at the same moment and beat the teak wood *kentongan* that hung from the lookout post at the village gate. There was a buzz of excitement in the crowd and Kancil watched as people craned their necks to see through the gate.

Someone came crashing through the trees below. Two boys were testing the tree trunks to find a way up to the canopy where Kancil and Kitchen Boy sat hidden by the thick foliage.

Kitchen Boy motioned for her to sit back against the branch to hide. He lay down flat on his branch and let out a low yowl that made Kancil's hair stand on end. At the same time, he threw a withered rambutan fruit to disturb the leaves of another branch, so when the boys looked up in terror, their eyes were drawn away from where Kancil and Kitchen Boy sat. Kitchen Boy yowled again. The boys didn't stay around to search the branches; they ran full pelt back to the north gate.

"How did you do that?" Kancil whispered when they had gone.

Kitchen Boy shrugged. "You pick up a few tricks in the forest," he said.

Kancil watched the parasol making slow, bumpy progress down the hill towards the village. As it drew closer, she could make out the square shape of the *jempana* carriage behind the parasol and as it drew closer still, the figures of the parasol bearer and the *jempana* bearers came into view. Light, golden fabric was draped over the roof of the carriage, obscuring her view of the prince.

When the prince's procession reached the lower terraced rice fields she could no longer see them above the village wall so she had to wait like everybody else for them to enter through the gate. The light was fading and men walked through the crowd, lighting lamps and bamboo torches. The long flickering shadows cast by the firelight gave the scene a ghostly feel. Kancil shivered.

"Are you cold?" asked Kitchen Boy. Kancil shook her head but she moved a little closer to him all the same. "Don't worry," Kitchen Boy grinned. "The bad spirits won't come near with everybody making so much noise."

The lookout rattled the *kentongan* and the *gamelan* music, which had been meandering in the background like a lazy buffalo, suddenly came together with four crashing beats as the bearers carried the *jempana* through the village gate.

The parasol bearer called out an order and the *jempana* was gently lowered to the ground. The villagers sat in silence as the curtain twitched and the prince emerged.

He wore a gold chest plate and gold armbands and over his *sarung* was a sash of fine ikat holding his *kris*, the ceremonial dagger, in place at his back. His shiny black hair was tied in a knot on top of his head and bound with a band bearing the Surya Majapahit seal.

Despite her intention to be unimpressed by the murderous Majapahit royalty, Kancil couldn't help admiring his regal poise and glittering finery. The most impressive thing about him, though, was surely his moustache. It was thick and glossy, such a contrast to the scrawny caterpillars that most men allowed to crawl under their noses. Kancil watched with a smile as Big Uncle's hand unconsciously reached up to cover his own facial hair.

The bearers moved the *jempana* away and a tall teak wood seat was brought for the prince to sit on. The musicians started up again and the dancers emerged one by one from behind the temple wall. They were dressed in plain *kain*, with indigo-dyed *kemben* wrapped tightly from armpits to hips to accentuate the taut bow shape of their bodies in their dancing poses.

Around each dancer's waist was a long sash of patterned cloth, the ends dyed a deep red that glowed in the flickering lamplight. The dancers moved with such tiny steps that they seemed to glide into position in two lines, their heads tipping from side to side in time with the music. Petals of beaten brass stood out on thin wires from their floral headdresses, moving as their heads tilted so it looked like tiny golden butterflies were flying above them.

The musicians beat a single note three times and Citra emerged from the temple, dressed just like the other dancers except for the silver thread woven through her *kemben*. She glided between the two rows to stand still in front of the prince for a heartbeat before bending her body like a leaf falling through the air to begin the dance.

The two lines of dancers parted to let Citra take the centre of the dance space. Her body was like a ribbon, weaving gracefully through the space, bending and gesturing towards the temple, towards the *pendopo*, towards the prince and towards the mountain. When she faced the *pendopo* she raised her head towards the tree where Kancil hid. For an instant their eyes met.

Kancil couldn't be sure that her cousin had actually seen her, but the expression on her face took Kancil's breath away – she looked so very sad. Then, with a flick of her patterned sash, Citra spun around to continue the dance. She was an excellent dancer.

"What have you got against Majapahit princes anyway?" Kitchen Boy asked.

"Eh?" said Kancil. The dance was over and the

speeches had begun. Big Uncle was mumbling and most people had stopped paying attention. Kancil had lost interest herself and was watching the crowd, although her eyes kept being drawn back to Citra, still in her dancing costume and sitting stiffly next to her father. If Citra had been a nicer person, Kancil would have felt sorry for her, sitting there trying not to look bored.

"Before," said Kitchen Boy, "you were moaning about having to look at a Majapahit prince like it was some big waste of your time."

"I wasn't moaning," Kancil replied.

"Well, whatever it was, you made out like you're the only girl in the village who's not excited about the prince coming here. So my guess is that secretly you're jealous of your cousin marrying the prince and you're trying to hide it by pretending you hate royalty."

"That's ridiculous," Kancil snapped. "For your information, your Majapahit king murdered my father. He also murdered the entire royal family of Sunda. It's possible that Bhre Mataram isn't as bloodthirsty as the king, but I'm not going to stick around to find out."

"Oh?" said Kitchen Boy. "Where are you going then?"

"I don't know," Kancil sighed. "Home to Sunda if I can. Definitely away from here. I can't stay mute for the rest of my life."

"And who will you go with?"

"If I can convince the *dalang* to take me as a servant, I'll go with his troupe as far as I can. If not, I'll go by myself."

"Now *that's* ridiculous," said Kitchen Boy.

"Why?"

"You're a girl, you can't go by yourself. And what about your mother? If you run away, who will look after her when she's old?"

Kancil had been trying not to think about how Mother fitted into her plans for escape. "She should never have brought me here," she said, "and in any case she'll be treated better if she doesn't have me with her, giving people like Bibi excuses to make snide remarks about bandit spawn." Kancil thought about the haunted house that had once been Bibi's home. It wasn't surprising that she was bitter, but that was no excuse for the way she treated people.

"And I *can* go by myself but if you'd like to come along, I'll consider taking you with me."

"Thank you for your kind offer," said Kitchen Boy, "but I quite like knowing where I'm going to sleep every night and I much prefer the predictable wrath of Bibi to taking my chances on the road."

"Suit yourself," said Kancil. She was a little disappointed that Kitchen Boy didn't want to join her.

At the same time, her disappointment was mixed with guilty relief. If she couldn't convince Mother to go with her, she would feel better about leaving her behind if Kitchen Boy was here.

Kitchen Boy leaned back against the tree trunk. "What about your brother?" he asked.

"What?" Kancil's head snapped around to face him.

"In the story your mother made up about Lawucilik, your father and brother were killed in the earthquake. You've said the king killed your father. You didn't say anything about your brother. You think he's still alive, don't you?"

"Maybe," Kancil said. She regretted confiding in Kitchen Boy now. She didn't want to talk to him about Agus. She knew he would point out the futility of trying to find him. But Kitchen Boy didn't mock her. "Perhaps you're right," he said, nodding his head slowly.

16

THE *JOGLO*

The next morning, Bibi shooed Kancil and Kitchen Boy out of the kitchen as soon as they had completed all the heavy chores for the day. "Go and make yourselves useful at the performers' lodgings," she ordered. Kancil knew this meant they would have to keep working while Bibi and Ida enjoyed a relaxing day, but she didn't mind. In fact, she was rather pleased that Bibi was inadvertently helping her plan to escape the village.

When they arrived at the house behind the north *pendopo*, the *dalang* had already gone to meditate in preparation for his dusk till dawn performance, but the other performers were all there. As Kitchen Boy had predicted, the singer greatly appreciated the cups of tea and shoulder massages that Kancil provided. When Dalang Mulyo lit the lamp at dusk to signal the beginning of the *wayang* performance, Kancil and Kitchen Boy were seated in the *pendopo* in prime position. They were directly behind the singer where they could watch the *dalang* bring the colourful flat-leather puppets to life from behind the shadow screen.

Before he began the performance, Dalang Mulyo turned around to make sure each of the performers was ready. When his gaze fell on Kancil and Kitchen Boy, he startled, as though noticing them for the first time. He looked first at Kitchen Boy, who stared cheekily back at him. Then the *dalang* looked at Kancil. She bowed her head but something made her change her mind and she raised her eyes to meet the *dalang*'s gaze. When he saw her eyes, his brow furrowed as though he was trying to remember something. He inclined his head in a slight nod before turning to face the shadow screen.

Kancil was still wondering what the *dalang*'s nod had meant the next morning as she swept the kitchen. She hoped she might be sent back to the performers' lodgings so she would have a chance to see him again. She knew it was foolish to think that he might have met Agus in Pekalongan and recognised the resemblance in her eyes. Even so, her mind kept leaping to that conclusion.

Her hopes of seeing the *dalang* again that morning were dashed when Bibi arrived at the kitchen.

"You're needed at the *joglo*," she snapped.

It was the first time Kancil had seen the *joglo*, which had been built on the foundations of the old Bhre Mataram's *joglo* just outside and a little uphill from the village. Twin stone shrines, built long before anybody could remember, stood like massive gateposts at the front of the courtyard. A high stone wall looped around the whole complex, from shrine to shrine, leaving only a narrow entrance at the front.

The old *joglo* had burned down when Mbah Merapi destroyed the village all those years ago. Inside the walled compound, only the stone guardians and the front steps, also made of stone, had survived. Giant teak trees had been dragged from the forest to become the pillars and roof joists of the new building. It was built in two parts: an open-air *pendopo* at the front and an enclosed *dalem* at the back. The smell of newly sawn timber hung in the air.

Ibu Tari was waiting for Kancil in the front courtyard near a clump of black bamboo that screened the *pendopo* from the front gate. She was anxiously clasping and unclasping her hands.

"I'm so relieved you're here," she said, ushering Kancil around to the kitchen at the back. "I don't know whether it was the excitement of the prince arriving or staying up all night to watch the *wayang*, but five women have decided to give birth today and the midwife can only be in one place at a time. I really must go and help."

Ibu Tari looked over towards the quiet *joglo*. She drew Kancil further into the kitchen and lowered her voice. "When the old Bhre used to come here, he always brought servants to manage the cooking and the cleaning. The village would provide help of course, but the royal servants would tell us when to enter the *joglo* and what meals to prepare. *These* ones though," she shook her head disapprovingly, "they're big strong boys who look good carrying a *jempana*. Apart from that all they're good at is eating and throwing spears."

She nodded towards a spike that had been set up in an open space. A pile of young coconuts with splintered husks lay around it. "You know, I don't think they're even up yet," she said as she slapped at a fly with a dishcloth. Kancil was in no doubt that if the prince's bearers had been Ibu Tari's own sons, it wouldn't be the fly that she was slapping.

At that moment, the back door of the *joglo* swung open and the parasol bearer emerged, sleepily scratching his belly. "Finally!" Ibu Tari murmured. "I'll tell him you're here then I'll be on my way. I'll be back soon, or I'll send someone to help, don't worry." With that, she walked out of the kitchen and over to the parasol bearer, hunching her shoulders and bowing her head politely.

"Sir, excuse me, sir," she said sweetly.

He grunted in reply. His hand moved from his belly to scratch his head, making his hair stand up on end.

"A girl is here to clean the *joglo*," Ibu Tari said, nodding towards the kitchen door where Kancil was standing. "Perhaps if you could tell her when His Highness goes to bathe so she can clean without being in the way. She doesn't speak, sir, but she understands and she's a hard worker. Now with your permission, sir, I will take my leave."

The parasol bearer looked over towards Kancil, and she quickly bowed her head.

When Ibu Tari left, the man went inside the *joglo* and silence returned. Presumably, the prince wasn't up yet and wouldn't be going to bathe any time soon. Kancil had the rare luxury of having absolutely nothing to do. She looked around the kitchen for somewhere comfortable to sit but the kitchen had not been designed for the comfort of servants so she wandered outside to explore the rear courtyard.

The kitchen and storerooms were on the north side of the courtyard and the latrine and pigsty butted up against the south wall. On the east wall a narrow gate was hidden behind a screen so nobody could see into the courtyard. Beyond the barred gate a deep ditch planted with spiky snake fruit bushes encircled the wall.

A narrow bridge spanned the ditch and provided the only access to the gate from the east forest. As she peered through the gate, Kancil had the feeling that someone was in the forest watching her. Rattled, she turned away and picked up the broom, hoping that sweeping would calm the uneasy feeling in her stomach.

The morning was disappearing and still there was no sign of movement from inside the *joglo*. The air was becoming hot and steamy and even though the sun was hidden behind clouds, Kancil could feel it beating down on her. She stowed her broom and went to sit in the shade cast by the *joglo*. She was beginning to doze when she was snapped back to wakefulness by the sound of someone breaking wind on the other side of the wall.

"Pwoar! That reeks!" a voice said.

"*Shhh!*" warned another.

"Ah," said the first, "the old lady's deaf and she's too busy bowing and scraping to notice anyway."

"The old lady's gone. There's a kid here now."

"Even better. You heard what Rat said, the kids here don't know anything."

"Keep your voices down," growled a third voice. "Don't take stupid risks."

Kancil was sitting bolt upright. She had to get to the kitchen before anyone came out or they would know she had heard. She shot across the courtyard and dived into the dark hut. She stared at the glowing coals under the rice steamer for a moment, trying to collect her thoughts. Could she have imagined it? No, it wasn't possible. There was no doubt in her mind that the first man had spoken in Sunda language. What was more, the way he said "bowing and scraping" revealed a particular dialect that Kancil used to hear often in the Muara Jati market. It was the dialect of pickpockets and tricksters.

Father used to be furious if he heard Kancil and Agus speaking the dialect, but Mother quietly encouraged them to pick up its nuances. "It doesn't hurt," she would tell Father, "to know what those low-lifes are saying. It's all right for you, out there on the sea with your honest crew. A woman needs to have her wits about her when she spends all day in the market."

Kancil tried to gather her thoughts as she picked up the broom again and started sweeping the kitchen that Ibu Tari had already swept spotless. It was unlikely, though still possible, that a Sunda market low-life could become the servant of a Majapahit prince. Father used to say they were like rats, always landing on their feet.

She was almost sure, though, that she recognised that first voice. It was hard to tell, because he had only given a short speech in polite Jawa at the welcome ceremony. Nevertheless, he had quite a distinctive voice and at the time she had thought that it went well with his glorious moustache. No matter how many ways she turned it around in her head, she couldn't come up with a way that a Sunda market low-life could become a Majapahit prince.

The rattling of the gate brought Kancil out of the kitchen. The prince and his men were struggling to undo the complicated locking system of the bars. Once the gate was open, five of the men, including the prince, walked out, presumably heading for the prince's bathing pool. The other three stayed behind to lock the gate. Kancil saw them stop and look through the gate towards the other end of the bridge, where she could faintly hear the five men talking – it sounded like they were greeting someone.

"What's *he* doing here?" she heard one of the men inside the gate say. This time there was no doubt that he was speaking Sunda language.

One of the men, who had a scar across his left cheek, clapped his hands to get Kancil's attention. "You," he called as he pointed to the *joglo*, "clean now!"

"No," moaned another, "tonic first. In there." He motioned for her to go back inside the kitchen. Kancil went in, hoping there would be some clue inside to help her figure out what sort of tonic he wanted.

"Four cups. *Pendopo*," he called after her.

Inside the kitchen, Kancil found raw rice soaking in

cold water. There was a jar of tamarind pulp, a plug of palm sugar and four *kencur* roots wrapped in a damp cloth. She set to work making *beras kencur* tonic. Four cups? she wondered. Who could the men have met on the other side of the bridge, and was it the same person she had sensed watching her earlier?

When she rounded the corner of the *pendopo* there were, indeed, four men sitting around a plate of sticky rice cakes. Their conversation stopped when she appeared. Kancil couldn't get a proper look at the newcomer because she was keeping her head bowed – only partly to be respectful. If they *were* Sunda market low-life, they might recognise her; some of the tricksters back home had got wise to the fact that she and Agus could understand them and would warn their friends to "watch out for the teak eyes".

"Clean now," Scar ordered when she had passed around the drinks. "Inside. Shut door."

Kancil shuffled backwards into the *dalem*, taking a broom that was leaning against the wall as she went.

"Whose brat is that?" someone asked. Strange, Kancil thought, he sounds like a local.

"Don't know," said the moaner, "but she makes good *jamu*."

"I hope she's not related to that crazy witch," said the local man.

"It's all right," said Scar, "she doesn't speak. Even so, you are a fool to come here. What if the old woman had been here? She might have recognised you."

"I'm not stupid," said the local indignantly. "I waited until I saw her leave, and I had to come here. There's a prob– Is she listening to us?"

Kancil realised too late that she was holding the broom in midair as she strained to hear them. If she started to sweep again now they would know she was listening. She hitched up her *kain* and in three desperate leaps made it to the other side of the room, offering up thanks to the village men for tying the floorboards firmly to the joists so they didn't squeak.

A partition divided the *dalem* into a front and a back room. By the time the local had got up and opened the front door, Kancil was behind the partition, her heart pounding.

"Must have gone out the back, lazy bint," she heard him say as he shut the door.

Strange, Kancil thought. That's what Bibi calls me. She didn't stop to wonder about it though. The man was talking more quietly and she could only hear snatches. She crept towards the door to hear better.

"... can't find it ... the well at the old house ... that damned *dalang* ..."

"We'll see what Bhre Mataram has to say when he

183

gets back," Scar said. "Now go to the kitchen and see if you can find that girl. I want some lime water, this *jamu* is sticking to my gut."

Kancil ran lightly across the floor and out the back door of the *dalem*. When the moaner came round the side of the house, she was halfway to the pigsty with a basket of slops on her head.

She made the lime water and tidied the *dalem*. Whenever she was near the men in the *pendopo* she tuned in to their conversation but she didn't hear any more useful information. She made another round of *beras kencur* for the five bathers when they returned and went to crouch on the ground beside the *pendopo* like she did for the village elders, ready to serve should they need any more drinks or something to eat. She hoped the local man would tell his story again.

There was a gap between the *pendopo* floor and the ground. The air under there had been insulated from the heat of the day and now a breeze was blowing from the other side of the *pendopo*, pushing out the cooler air from under the floor towards Kancil. She had just manoeuvred herself to get maximum benefit from the cool breeze when the parasol bearer leaned over the edge of *pendopo*. "You can go now," he said, "we won't need you any more."

17

SPIES

When she returned to the kitchen shortly before the midday meal, Kancil hoped she would find Kitchen Boy alone. He was the only person she could talk to about what she had heard at the *joglo*.

It was a vain hope: Kitchen Boy was nowhere to be seen and both Bibi and Ida were there. Bibi's forehead was stuck all over with patches of *jamu* paste to draw out the bad air causing her head to ache. The patches didn't appear to be working very well because Bibi was in an even fouler mood than usual.

Each household took it in turns to feed the workers in the field. Today was Bibi's turn. She stomped around and threw things as though this duty had been designed specifically to make her life difficult. Even Ida became fed up with her. "Your head would ache less if you didn't shout so much," she said under her breath.

"You'll keep your mouth *shut*," Bibi retorted, throwing a hunk of coconut husk at her. It caught a gourd of coconut milk that was sitting by the stove, spilling its contents all over the floor.

"You clumsy fool," said Bibi.

"It was *your* fault," Ida shouted back.

The morning continued like that. Kancil was relieved when Bibi told her to take the tray of food to the workers.

When she arrived at the *pondok*, where her shell necklace once lay hidden, she discovered that Kitchen Boy was taking his turn at working in the field. He arrived at the *pondok* with a basket of rice paddy snails just as she got there. Two other village boys were with him. One carried a hoe and the other a basket of weeds. They rinsed their muddy legs at the water barrel that stood near the *pondok* steps then set about devouring the rice and greens Kancil had brought them, without even a glance in her direction.

Kancil's stomach grumbled loudly and the boys looked up.

"Isn't she the dumb girl who works in your kitchen?" one of the boys asked Kitchen Boy.

He nodded. "Her stomach's not so quiet though," he said.

"Here, girl, you can eat with us," said the other boy, making room for her.

Kancil joined them gratefully. When the meal was finished, the village boys rolled onto their backs to sleep. Kitchen Boy reached for the *kendi* to take a swig of water.

"Bah! Empty!" he said. "Come on." He motioned for Kancil to join him as he stood up. "Walk with me to the spring."

"That *kendi*'s not empty," said Kancil when they were out of earshot. She had been the last to drink from it.

"I know, but you wanted to talk to me," Kitchen Boy replied.

"How could you tell?" she asked, astounded.

Kitchen Boy shrugged. "I could tell by looking at you," he said. "What's up?"

Kancil filled him in as quickly as she could; they had already reached the spring.

"You're not certain it was the prince you heard speaking like a thief?" he asked when she had finished.

Kancil shook her head.

"So it's possible that he is who he says he is but he's got bad taste in servants?"

Kancil nodded slowly. "But," she said, "even if he is a prince, he's up to something. He must know they're Sunda low-lifes; they were speaking openly in front of him. And then there's the local man – there was something not right about him."

"There's only one thing for it," said Kitchen Boy. "We're going to have to spy on them."

"How?" Kancil asked.

"I'll figure something out. What sort of a mood is Bibi in today?"

"Bad, she has a headache."

"Interesting," said Kitchen Boy, stroking his chin thoughtfully. "I think I have an idea. Leave it to me."

"I know the perfect *jamu* for you. It will cure that head in an instant."

Kitchen Boy had returned from the fields and was preparing the snails he had collected, scooping the meat out of the shells and skewering it on sharpened bamboo sticks. Bibi was hunched in the corner near the fire. Rain poured down all around and she complained that she felt like it was drumming into her head. Kancil made her a ginger tea then retreated to the narrow verandah at the front of the kitchen where Ida had already wisely moved – it was far enough away to be safe from Bibi's throwing arm.

Bibi grunted in reply to Kitchen Boy's suggestion. Undeterred by her response, he continued, "The problem is, it requires dusk lily buds."

"Never heard of such a thing," Bibi scoffed.

"They're not very common and they have to be picked at dusk to be effective," Kitchen Boy continued. "I know where they grow, deep in the forest. I'm happy to collect some for you. I'll have the *jamu* ready first thing in the morning. I'll need help, though. Perhaps Ida would come with me?"

"Forget it," said Ida. "You won't catch me in the forest at night, take the girl."

"Is that all right, Bibi?" Kitchen Boy asked.

"I don't care what you do," she groaned. "Just make sure the stupid bint doesn't get eaten by a tiger or I'll never hear the end of it."

Bint, thought Kancil. That had been Bibi's name for her ever since she got in trouble for calling her bandit spawn. And someone else had said it recently. Kancil had a feeling it was important, but she couldn't remember who it was.

"Is there really such a thing as a dusk lily?" Kancil asked when they were a safe distance from the village.

"Not as far as I know," Kitchen Boy replied.

"So what will you tell Bibi when you don't have *jamu* for her?"

"Oh, I'll have *jamu* for her. If I tell her it has dusk lily in it, she'll believe me."

As they got closer to the *joglo*, Kancil thought of more and more reasons why spying on the prince was a bad idea. "Wouldn't we have been better to stay at Big Uncle's and listen in to the elders meeting at the *pendopo*?" she whispered to Kitchen Boy. "Perhaps they know something that we don't."

Kitchen Boy stopped and looked at her. "Don't be stupid," he said. "*You're* the only person in this place who knows *anything*."

The compliment didn't make her feel proud, it made her anxious. What if she had made a mistake? Imagined the whole thing? What would happen to her if she were caught spying on a prince? What would happen to Mother?

She regretted telling Kitchen Boy about her suspicions. She was supposed to be working on the *dalang* to help her get out of here, not racing around trying to solve the mystery of the prince's true identity. How was this going to help her find Agus?

They stepped off the path and into the forest. It was difficult walking through the undergrowth. The concentration required to avoid touching itchy weed or thorn bushes while walking soundlessly distracted Kancil from thinking about her impending doom.

Nearer to the *joglo* they could see the soft glow of a lamp shining from the *pendopo* and hear the rumble of quiet conversation. They edged round the wall to the back gate. Kitchen Boy tested the bars and chose a spot where he thought he could squeeze through. Kancil caught his wrist. "You'll get stuck," she hissed.

"I might not," he replied.

"Well, then, *I'll* get stuck," she said, "and even if we do get through, there's nowhere to hide in there. If one of them comes around the back, we'll be caught for sure."

"You got a better idea?"

Kancil thought a better idea would be to scurry back to Big Uncle's home as fast as possible. She didn't think that would be a good way to convince Kitchen Boy to give up his crazy scheme, though.

"Around the front," she said instead. "It's dark now so they won't see us if we sneak through the front gate and we can hide in the black bamboo in the courtyard. I think we'll be able to hear them from there and if they get suspicious we can make a run for it out through the front. If we're quick enough, they'll think we're a couple of monkeys looking for scraps."

Kitchen Boy grinned. "You're actually quite good at this sneaking around, spying on people business, aren't you?"

"No," Kancil whispered back, "I just don't want to get caught."

They slipped around the front gate and crouched in

the bamboo. The men were gathered in the *pendopo*, passing around a flask made from a long bamboo tube and taking turns to drink from it. Kancil had seen flasks like that used for storing *tuak* palm wine.

The black bamboo was a good hiding place, but Kancil discovered a flaw in her plan as she strained to listen – the men were being more cautious now that it was dark so they were speaking quietly. She would have to move closer if she wanted to hear what they were saying.

"If I can get close to the *joglo*, I can slip under the edge of the *pendopo* floor in the gap I noticed when I was waiting on the men earlier," she whispered.

The problem was getting to the *joglo*: she would be out of sight if she hid behind one of the two stone guardians in front of the steps, but there was no way to get from the bamboo to the guardian or from the guardian to the *joglo* without being in the open long enough for someone to see her.

"Can you distract them?" She pointed towards the wall on the other side of the courtyard. "Throw a stone or something over there so they all look that way for a moment, to give me time to get under the *pendopo*." She couldn't quite believe that she was suggesting this. Kitchen Boy looked at her with admiration.

"I have a better idea," he whispered back. "I'll be able

to get you under there, but you'll have to find your own way out. I'm sure you've already thought of that, haven't you?"

Kancil chewed her lip. "I guess I'll be stuck there until they all go to sleep, or go inside. What if they post a guard at the gate? I'll be stuck there all night! I'll have to pretend somehow to arrive with Ibu Tari in the morning. I take it back; it was a stupid idea."

"Pah!" said Kitchen Boy. "Now you're thinking too much. If you always thought about what *might* happen, you'd never do anything. You'll need to come up with an idea for escape. I'll be at the *pondok*. If I don't see you there by dawn, I'll come back and get you." And before Kancil could stop him, he leaped up and darted out the front gate.

"What was that?" one of the men said, clearly enough for her to hear. The men looked up.

"Monkey," said another and the quiet conversation resumed.

18

GOLD

Kancil waited behind the bamboo. She was beginning to wonder if Kitchen Boy was playing a cruel trick on her when she heard a long rumbling growl followed by the shriek of terrified monkeys. A moment later Kitchen Boy dashed through the gate, waving a stick in his good arm. He ran straight up the steps and scooted around to the far side of the *pendopo*, falling to his knees and bowing to the floor.

The men leaped up. Some were looking over the wall, towards where the growl and shrieks had come from, and others were staring at the strange figure at their feet. All were looking in the opposite direction to where Kancil was. She saw her opportunity, dashed across the courtyard and squeezed herself into the gap under the *pendopo* floor.

"Forgive me, Bhre," she heard Kitchen Boy wail. "The mighty tiger was not pleased with me collecting *jamu* in his forest at night. I beg you let me stay near the safety of your lamp until he loses interest in teaching me a lesson."

"A tiger? Really?" Kancil recognised Scar's voice. "I'd like to see that. Fatty, light that torch. Let's go and take a look. Come on, boy, you can show us where he is."

"I'd really rather not," said Kitchen Boy in a squeaky voice.

"What?" roared Scar. "You'll do what you're told!"

"Oh, leave him be," said the parasol bearer. "Can't you see the kid's terrified?"

Kancil had never heard a tiger's growl so she didn't know what it should sound like. The growl in the forest had convinced the monkeys, though, and Kitchen Boy was making a very good show of being scared. Yet it must have been him mimicking a tiger – it was too much of a coincidence that a tiger should appear moments after he went looking for a way to distract the men. Kancil remembered Kitchen Boy's story about meeting his tiger spirit in the forest. Her skin prickled.

"I've lit this torch now," someone said. "We might as well go and have a look." The floor creaked and through the gaps between the floorboards Kancil could see two men descend the steps and walk towards the front gate.

One of them was Scar and the other was the tallest and skinniest of the *jempana* bearers. Kancil guessed that he must be Fatty.

"Why were you collecting *jamu* at night?" the parasol bearer asked Kitchen Boy.

Kitchen Boy explained about the dusk lilies and elaborated with a list of other medicinal plants that were more potent when harvested at night. He went on to tell them about various close encounters he had had with tigers over the years. Kancil willed him to be quiet and let the men get on with their conversation. She hadn't folded herself into this cramped hole to listen to Kitchen Boy show off.

As Kitchen Boy prattled on, Kancil heard a soft whistle from behind the building. One of the men muttered, "That'll be him. Get rid of the boy," in Sunda language before thumping down the steps and around the side of the building.

"Time for you to go home to bed now, kid," the parasol bearer said. "Sounds like your tiger's gone elsewhere anyway."

"I thank you most humbly for your protection," Kitchen Boy said in polite Jawa language. Kancil smiled. She had taught him that phrase.

When Kitchen Boy left, Kancil suddenly felt very vulnerable. Don't be stupid, she told herself, you were no safer with him up there than you are now. A part of her was still in shock at her decision to spy on the prince but mostly, despite the fear, she felt exhilarated. She realised now how much she missed the comings and goings at the market in Muara Jati, where she used to help Mother most days. Whenever a new boat pulled in at the harbour, there would be different faces to look at, languages to listen to. Here, every day was the same, everybody looked the same, sounded the same. Until now.

Two pairs of legs passed by her hiding place and the timber above her head groaned as the men sat down. Carefully, she eased herself back towards the edge of the *pendopo*, further away from the light of the lamp.

"Rat! What took you so long?" the prince demanded. It was *definitely* the prince and he was *definitely* talking the thieves' dialect.

"Don't call me that." It was the local man Kancil had seen that morning.

"Why not?" asked the prince. "You're just like a rat, sneaky and clever. That's a compliment where I come from." The men all laughed loudly. They had been passing around the *tuak* and were a lot more relaxed now. Kancil suspected she would have been able to hear them from the hiding place in the bamboo.

"Anyway, what's the news?" the prince continued.

At that moment Scar and Fatty rounded the front gate.

"Where's that kid?" asked Scar.

"Gone," said the parasol bearer. "What's your problem?"

"I'd like to see where that tiger was, is all," Scar grumbled. "Couldn't even find footprints and we searched all over."

"What kid?" asked Rat.

"Some kid out collecting *jamu* in the forest got spooked by a tiger and came running in here. Don't worry, we sent him on his way."

"Cripple?" asked Rat.

"Possibly. Might have had something wrong with one of his arms. Why? Do you know him?"

"No, but that witch I told you about – the one who used to spy on us in the forest – I heard a rumour she was training up some cripple who was supposed to be a tiger charmer."

Suddenly, Kancil remembered what had been troubling her – the local man had called her a bint, and now she thought about it, he sounded a bit like Bibi when he spoke. Could he be Bibi's son, the scoundrel? And if he *was* the scoundrel, were these the bandits who had stolen the temple treasure all those years ago?

"We'd better be careful," the prince said. "Do you think she might have sent him to spy on us? Are you sure he's gone? Go check to make sure he's not hiding near the gate. Go on, Itam, do something useful for a change."

Kancil watched as the man she had nicknamed the moaner lumbered down the steps and peered out into the darkness beyond the wall. "No sign," he said when he came back, "and even if he was here, he wouldn't understand us."

"Maybe not, but *she* might. She's cunning, that witch. She might have sent him to distract us while she slipped in through the back," said the local man.

"All right, go and check," the prince sighed. "Doesn't hurt to be careful."

Kancil held her breath and curled herself up into as small a ball as she could. She had recognised this as a perfect hiding spot straightaway this morning. What if they did the same? If they looked under the *pendopo*, she was done for.

She heard the men stomping around outside and through the *dalem*. "No sign," Itam said when they returned. "If you ask me, Rat's making us jumpy on purpose."

"And why would I do that?" the local man snarled.

"Because you messed up. You can't find it, can you?"

"Eh?" said Rat.

With each swig of *tuak* the bandits had slipped

further into their Sunda low-life dialect. Kancil had to concentrate hard to understand them and she guessed the scoundrel was also struggling.

"You … can't … find … the … gold," Itam repeated.

"It's not *my* fault," Rat whined. "The mountain's a completely different shape to what it was before it blew, and the trees I used as markers have all gone. Anyway, I told you: if someone can get into the old house to get my stick, I'll be able to find the gold no problem."

"You and your precious stick," Itam snorted.

"Enough of this," the prince snapped. "Remember what we're all here for."

No! thought Kancil. Don't just remember. Say it! Stop talking in riddles! Her legs were starting to cramp. She was more than ready for them to reveal their secret so she could get out of there.

"I don't understand how a stick hidden down a well is going to help us find the gold," said Itam.

"He's been through that, Itam. Are you deaf?" asked the parasol bearer wearily. "He goes to a secret place and holds up his stick and where the end of the stick points is exactly where the gold is. Right, Rat?"

"It's a bit more complicated than that," said Rat. "There are notches and I have to hold it up in different ways to get the lines to meet up. But in essence, that's it. You get me that stick and I'll find the gold. If you mess with me, though, I'll break the stick and you'll get nothing."

The men were quiet as they passed the *tuak* around.

"What you're forgetting, Rat," said the prince, "is that gold or no gold we stand to do quite nicely out of this little venture so long as we all keep our wits about us. So calm down and don't go doing anything stupid."

"So long as you honour your promise," Rat grumbled. "You can do what you want with the rest of them but keep my mother and my sister out of it."

"Of course, dear Rat," said the prince. His voice was smooth and mellow but there was something about it that made Kancil think of a snake. "Though I think I've figured out which one of that buffoon's household is your mother," the prince continued, "and I can't say I understand your devotion. What are you going to do with the old hag? She'll be your responsibility you know, once we've—"

The prince was cut off in mid-sentence and the *pendopo* shook as someone lunged across the floor. From the noises, Kancil guessed that Rat had the prince by the throat. The lamplight flickered as other men rose to their feet and joined the scuffle. A confusion of thumps and grunts and groans followed. Then there was a particularly loud thump and a body crashed to the floor.

"Is he all right?" Fatty asked.

"He will be when he wakes up," said the parasol bearer. "Now where's that *tuak*?"

Very slowly, so as not to make a sound, Kancil stretched out along the ground to stop the numbness that was creeping into her legs. So there was gold buried somewhere – could it be the temple treasures? Small Aunt said the *juru kunci* saw the scoundrel handing the treasure over to the bandits. Perhaps the *juru kunci* was confused and it was actually the bandits handing over the treasure to the scoundrel to bury.

Kancil tried to remember exactly what Small Aunt had told her. She was so tired she was finding it hard to concentrate. She yawned and blinked her eyes, trying to stay awake. Think about that later, she told herself. Right now, you've got to listen for clues to what the Rat meant when he said "you can do what you want with the rest of them".

Kancil woke with such a start that she jumped and her head banged against a floorboard. The conversation above her stopped. "What was that?" the parasol bearer asked.

"There's something under the floor."

The men kneeled on the floor to peer between the boards. Kancil could smell the *tuak* on their breath and was grateful that the alcohol had made them clumsy, so that they kept blocking their own light.

"Can't see anything," the prince slurred. "Go down there and have a look."

Somebody took a lamp and stomped down the steps. In a desperate move, Kancil wedged herself against a floor beam, hoping that the lamplight would shine past her. She rolled onto something furry. It scurried out from under her with a squeal and for a moment the realisation that she had almost squashed a rat with her own body outweighed her fear of discovery.

She managed to stop herself from scrambling out from under the *pendopo*. That was what the rat did – just as Itam bent down with the lamp to inspect the underfloor space.

"Ugh! A rat!" he exclaimed, leaping backwards.

"Wha …?" Rat woke up to the sound of his name. The others all roared with laughter and the noise under the floorboards was forgotten. Kancil rubbed at the bump on her head. She was wide awake now.

Somebody went inside the *dalem*. Kancil heard something wooden clatter to the floor above her. "There's your precious stick," the parasol bearer said.

"When did you find that?" Rat grabbed at the stick.

"Never mind that," the parasol bearer replied. "Now, you'll take that stick and figure out where the treasure is, but you're not going to dig anything up until we get there. Red and Tor will go with you to keep you honest." Two of the bearers rose to their feet.

"We'll be at the meeting place at sundown a week from today," the prince said. "We don't want you coming anywhere near here or the village until then, do you hear?"

Rat grunted in reply.

"You've got a week, Rat." It was the parasol bearer speaking again. "That's five days. Can you count to five?"

Rat muttered something under his breath.

"Your mother will be with us. You know what will happen if you're not there. Or if anything is missing. Now go!" said the parasol bearer.

When the scoundrel and the two bearers had gone, the others settled back to drink more *tuak*.

"The wedding is settled, then?" Fatty ventured.

"Yes," the prince sighed. "It took some work to convince the priest that three days from today is an auspicious date. And it's lucky for us the *juru kunci* was away talking to his mountain spirits all day. Those two aren't as stupid as the girl's father and the other one. Anyway, it's all arranged. They think that every able-bodied villager is leaving with us in a week to help me present my bride to the king at the full moon festival in Trowulan. I hope you all appreciate the sacrifices I'm making for you. These people are insufferable."

Itam, who Kancil had noticed always seemed to be given the worst jobs, spoke up now. "What's so difficult about acting like royalty all day?" he grumbled.

The prince turned on him. "I *am* royalty, and don't you forget it!" he snarled. "Just because my father fell out with the old Queen Tribhuwana and lost his rightful position, doesn't change the fact that I have royal blood. I can't wait to see the look on the king's face when we take the Majapahit Palace. My cousin, *King* Hayam Wuruk! What a joke!"

Scar cleared his throat. "Are there really enough men in this village to take Trowulan?" he asked.

"We'll take Salatiga first to boost our numbers," the prince replied. "It will only take a fraction of our gold to buy the cooperation of those who matter there. And don't forget, the tiger stone is with the hoard. With its power we can't lose."

Kancil caught her breath. She should have quizzed Kitchen Boy when he asked if her father had mentioned the tiger stone.

"Forgive me, Bhre, but are you sure?" Fatty asked. "Trowulan is the capital; it will be crawling with soldiers and we can't be certain about the tiger stone. That holy man seemed a bit mad to me, the one who told us that the tiger stone would give you power over wild beasts. It's a nice idea to have a tiger at your side in battle, but wouldn't it be better to take the gold back to a Sunda port to sell? Nobody would ask questions there and we'd be nicely set up. You could rule all the trade in Nusantara. You'd be rich beyond your dreams."

"I don't want to be *rich*!" fumed the prince. "I'm not going to spend the rest of my life watching over pirate rabble in some stinking port. I'm going to avenge my father's honour and I'm going to be the King of Majapahit."

"Again, Bhre, forgive me," Fatty continued. "None of us doubts your right to the throne, but these people, they're farmers, not soldiers. How will they defeat the king's guard?"

"They won't," the prince replied. "Don't underestimate these yokels, though. They're a proud bunch and when I whisper in a certain doting father's ear, all the insulting things the king's guard have said about Princess Citra, his blood will boil. He'll fire his people up to fight for her honour. We'll let them make a bit of a show then we come from behind to put down the Mataram rebellion. My dear cousin, the so-called king, will be full of gratitude and grant me a private audience. It's only a well-judged knife throw then, between me and the throne."

"It is a masterful plan, Bhre," the parasol bearer spoke for the first time since sending the scoundrel on his way. "We must make sure that the *dalang* and his troupe go back to Pekalongan as soon as they have performed the *wayang* for the wedding. We don't want them getting in the way."

Kancil lay in her cramped hiding place, taking in what she had just heard. She quite liked the part where the prince knifed King Hayam Wuruk, the king responsible for her own father's murder, but it was the plan of a madman.

Mad or not, the prince had a hold over the other bandits and he would soon have a hold over Big Uncle. It was easy to imagine Big Uncle, with his pompous vanity and his poor command of polite Jawa language, being tricked into going along with the prince until it was too late.

If Kancil left with the *dalang*'s troupe, as she hoped to do, she would save herself. Yet how could she possibly do that, knowing what she knew? The prince had to be stopped, but how?

The faint light in the sky told her that it would soon be dawn. The men had fallen silent, then each in turn had started to snore. She waited until she could hear six different sleepers before she carefully uncurled and crawled out from under the floor. She took a moment to rub the life back into her legs, all the while straining her ears for the slightest sound, then she stood up.

It was still so dark that she could only make out the broad shape of the black bamboo and the outline of the shrines.

If anybody is awake, she told herself, they won't know it's me unless they catch me. They would know someone had been spying on them, though.

Kancil didn't want their suspicion falling on Small Aunt and Kitchen Boy – she had no doubt that the prince would use his influence over Big Uncle to make them suffer if he wanted to.

She stepped out of the shadow of the *pendopo* and began to walk slowly towards the front gate. Her heart was beating wildly and every nerve in her body told her to run, yet she forced herself to keep her back straight and take small even steps so she might look as though she were floating. If any of the men did catch sight of her, she wanted them to think she was a spirit. They might be big scary bandits, but even bandits would think twice about approaching a spirit in the middle of the night.

19

A PLAN

"They're bandits," said Kancil when she had reached the *pondok* and shaken Kitchen Boy awake. "They might even be the same bandits that Small Aunt told us about, the ones who used to play dice games in the forest, the ones who led the scoundrel astray."

Kitchen Boy's eyes widened.

"And speaking of the scoundrel – he's alive."

Kitchen Boy's mouth dropped open. Kancil wished she wasn't so tired. As it was, she couldn't properly enjoy the pleasure of shocking him.

"That's not possible," he said. "Ibu Jamu said he sacrificed himself to Mbah Merapi."

Kancil shook her head. "She said he was last seen walking towards the mountain as everybody else was running away. He must have tricked them, doubled back or something. I don't think anyone would take the time to make certain he'd burned to death when they were all busy saving themselves.

"In any case, he's alive and they call him Rat *and* he's buried some gold somewhere. I think it's the gold that they stole from the temple and he's on his way to find it again now. But they're planning something much worse than stealing the temple treasures …"

Kancil told Kitchen Boy everything she had heard.

"Are you sure that's what they said about the tiger stone?"

"Yes," Kancil replied. "What do you know about it?"

"Well," said Kitchen Boy, "that holy man I told you about, the one I met in the temple. He told me a story about the tiger stone. If it was the same holy man, then I think he told the bandits a different story to the one he told me."

"What did he tell you?" Kancil was growing impatient. "You thought it had something to do with my father."

"He told me that he met a trader at the temple many years ago. The trader was meditating at the temple because a precious stone had been stolen from him and he wanted the spirits' advice about what to do. The trader called it the tiger stone and said that it had been passed down to him from his father and his father's father and so on.

"The trader's father told him that the stone had special powers but he didn't know what they were. The trader came from a long line of sons and the family legend said that only a daughter could unlock the stone's power."

"What made you think the trader was my father?" Kancil asked.

"Your eyes. The way they reminded me of my tiger spirit. Tiger eyes, tiger spirit, tiger stone. It all seemed like too much of a coincidence. The bandit was right about the holy man though: he was a bit mad. So who knows what the real story is?"

Kancil was silent, thinking. If Father *was* the trader who had met the holy man, perhaps he had told him the story of his father coaxing the tiger away from the village. When the holy man told the bandits that the stone would give its owner power over wild beasts, perhaps he got the story muddled up, or perhaps he lied to them for reasons of his own.

She remembered the puzzle that had been playing on her mind since that day she dreamed of her shell necklace sinking into the mud: the scoundrel, the temple treasure, Agus. She was sure her father's spirit had given her that dream and there must be a reason why he had put those three thoughts together for her.

Perhaps the scoundrel had stolen the stone from

Father and hidden it with the temple treasure. If that was true, then *she* was the daughter who could unlock the stone's power. Perhaps Father's spirit knew what that power was now. Could it be that the stone could somehow lead her to Agus? She remembered what Father had murmured on the beach when he gave her the shell necklace: "What is lost is lost." Could he have been talking about the tiger stone?

Don't be stupid, she told herself. Father never said anything about a tiger stone and he *loved* talking about tigers. It was much more likely that the tiger stone was a story made up by a charlatan posing as a holy man to coax food and drink out of fellow travellers. Wondering about it was distracting her from coming up with a plan to stop her cousin from marrying the prince.

"What should we do now?" Kitchen Boy broke the silence.

"You're asking *me*?" Kancil was incredulous.

"Yes," he said, "why not?"

"Because you're usually the one with all the ideas and I've just spent the night stuck in a hole in the ground. It's your turn to think of something."

"We could wait until the bandits dig up the treasure then steal the tiger stone from them. Then you do whatever it is you have to do with it to harness its power to save the village."

Kancil stared at him. "What you're saying is, if I want a *sensible* plan to stop the bandits, then I'll have to think of it myself?"

Kitchen Boy laughed. "I guess so," he said.

"We're not sure the tiger stone is real and stopping the bandits from getting away with the treasure isn't the most important thing. The most important thing is to stop the wedding," she said.

"I thought perhaps you might take some pleasure in seeing your darling cousin married off to a bandit," said Kitchen Boy.

"She's a pain, but she doesn't deserve that," Kancil said. She was thinking about the look on her cousin's face when their eyes met at the welcome dance. That look had told her they did have something in common; they were both trapped. "Anyway, it's not only her we have to save. If the wedding goes ahead, then the whole village is in danger. I can't speak, so you'll have to tell Big Uncle what I overheard."

"That won't work," said Kitchen Boy. "He'll only consider an idea if it comes from someone important or if he thinks it was his idea in the first place."

Kancil was so tired now that she was beginning to see phantom bandits climbing over the edge of the *pondok*. She shook her head. "I have to sleep," she said and stretched out on the floor.

"We should go back to the village," Kitchen Boy said, trying to pull her upright. "It will be light soon."

"No," Kancil said firmly. "I'm going to sleep now. Wake me when you can see who is asleep in the lookout post."

"It's Eko." Kitchen Boy was shaking Kancil to wake up.

"What?" she asked sleepily.

"It's Eko on lookout duty. He's not asleep any more so we're going to have to explain ourselves." He held up some weeds he had collected in the forest. "Bibi sent us to collect dusk lily. It rained. We took shelter in the *pondok* and fell asleep. Lucky for us it did rain last night. Come on, I'd better get back and make some kind of a concoction for Bibi's head."

Kancil didn't move. She was watching a wisp of smoke rising from somebody's kitchen fire.

"The smoking *jamu* that you put in the jar in the kitchen – is it still there?"

Kitchen Boy nodded. He looked puzzled. "I didn't think you wanted anything more to do with that after what happened with your mother," he said.

Kancil ignored him. "Can you get hold of a brazier and the smoking *jamu* and meet me behind the pavilion where Big Uncle sleeps after everyone has gone to bed tonight?"

"Maybe …" Kitchen Boy was looking at her sideways, a teasing grin forming on his lips.

"Are you going to help me save the village or not?" Kancil snapped.

"Of course, madam," he said, bowing deeply before her. "I assume I would be foolish to expect any kind of explanation in advance as to my role in saving the village?"

"You assume correctly," Kancil replied.

Kitchen Boy was looking thoughtful. "There are some things I have to do in the forest this evening. I'll be back before your uncle starts snoring."

"I wish I knew how you manage to come and go as you please without getting into trouble," Kancil said.

Kitchen Boy shrugged. "It's just the way it is," he said. "Freedom to come and go as I please has its advantages. The other side of it is that if I go and don't come back, nobody's likely to come looking for me."

"*I'd* come looking for you," Kancil said.

"Thanks," said Kitchen Boy.

Was there a remnant of the necklace under the *pondok* that gave me the idea while I slept? Kancil wondered. Or was it Mother's practical market sense — making do with what is at hand? Either way, if this plan is to succeed, I'll have to live up to my name — Kancil, the mouse deer, the clever little creature who uses words to outwit the bigger, stronger creatures. And be careful to use the right language! Kancil smiled as she imagined what Small Aunt would have to say about her plan.

Mother didn't seem wholly convinced by Kancil's explanation for having stayed out all night but she didn't question her. Kancil was on the verge of confiding in her but she stopped herself. What had seemed like a good idea out in the *pondok* with Kitchen Boy by her side and the sun rising on a fresh new day was feeling as shaky as their little sleeping shack now she was in her uncle's home. She couldn't take the risk of Mother talking her out of it. She didn't have the time, anyway. She could hear Bibi stomping down the passageway.

Time moved slowly that day. Kancil managed to sneak in a couple of much-needed naps in the morning, suffering only one stinging ear from Bibi as a consequence. She rehearsed her plan over and over in her head and by the afternoon she was so distracted that she burned a dish of *kangkung* greens. This earned her a proper beating from Bibi and she resolved to put the plan out of her mind until nightfall.

The elders met that evening as usual in Big Uncle's *pendopo*. The *juru kunci* had returned from the mountain. "The spirits are uneasy," he said.

Kancil pricked up her ears. Perhaps the *juru kunci*

was wise to the bandits' plot. Maybe he would save her from having to follow through on her plan.

Big Uncle frowned. "Once the marriage has taken place, our village will have royal protection and in time that will drive the bandit curse from the forest. Surely that will please the spirits."

The *juru kunci* looked down at his hands and said nothing. Holy men, Kancil decided, had their limitations.

"What's more," Big Uncle continued, "the prince has sent two of his bearers for reinforcements. Within a week of us leaving for the capital, he has promised there will be a garrison of soldiers here to protect those left behind from any bandit threat. There will be nothing more to do here than keep the birds away from the rice fields and we'll be back in time for harvest."

Kancil's heart sank. The prince was too clever for her. He would make sure that Big Uncle didn't have any doubts until it was too late.

"There is one matter we need to discuss," Big Uncle said, a little unwillingly. "The prince's men heard a tiger near the *joglo* last night. I offered to send some young men to see it off but the prince wishes to hunt it himself tomorrow."

"You will accompany him?" asked the priest.

"I guess I must," said Big Uncle.

"You will take the kitchen boy, won't you?" asked the *juru kunci*.

"Hmpf," Big Uncle grumbled, "if we can find him, that little pest. He has a talent for disappearing at the very moment he's needed."

"It would be wise to take him."

"As bait?" asked Big Uncle.

"As protection," the *juru kunci* replied.

When her evening chores were complete, Kancil returned to the shack where Mother was waiting. The worst of Mother's illness had passed but she was still quite weak. She couldn't walk more than a few steps without resting.

At least I know they won't take her to Trowulan, Kancil thought, they'll leave her here to keep the birds off the rice field. An image came to her mind of her mother and all the others left behind, waiting. Waiting until they starved, or until bandits took the village, or until word came of what their kin were believed to have done in Trowulan. They would die of shame if that happened.

My plan has to work, she told herself. And I have to make sure that Mother doesn't try to stop me from doing what I have to do tonight.

"Mother," she whispered when she was sure they were alone, "do you remember when we left Sunda and we had to go in the boat, and I was scared and you said

I shouldn't ask questions and everything would all be all right?"

"Mmm," said Mother.

"I did what you said, didn't I?"

"Yes," Mother agreed. She was looking at Kancil closely in the moonlight.

"*Did* you know that everything would be all right?"

"No."

"But did me not asking questions make it seem more likely that everything *would* be all right?"

Mother laughed softly at this. "Yes," she said, "I admit that believing you trusted me made me trust myself a little more."

"And you remember how Kitchen Boy and I made you well with Small Aunt's *jamu*?"

"Yes," said Mother. She was frowning now, trying to work out where Kancil's questions were going.

"Well, we have to do something a bit like that tonight. It has to be very secret for a reason I can't explain. So please don't ask any questions and everything will be all right."

Mother was silent for a while then she said, "You're not going to run away, are you?"

Kancil chose her words carefully. "I'm not going to run away tonight," she said, "but one day I will have to leave this place.

20

WHISPERING SPIRITS

Kancil crept along the passageway at the side of the main house, holding her breath in fear of waking one of the sleepers within. When she reached the front of the house she checked to see if anyone was on the verandah. She was relieved to find it empty. In the moonlight, she could see Big Uncle's feet sticking out of the pavilion, just like last time, but she couldn't hear a sound – perhaps he was still awake, fretting about the tiger hunt.

She crouched down and sprinted across the open courtyard to the darkness behind the pavilion. Kitchen Boy was already there. He had a palm leaf fan in his hand, and the *jamu* was at his feet, but there was no brazier. Kancil looked at him in alarm. He nodded towards the fence. When Kancil peered into the darkness she could see a faint glow of burning charcoal – Kitchen Boy had lit the brazier far enough away that Big Uncle wouldn't notice the heat or the smell of burning before he went to sleep.

Kitchen Boy cocked his head towards the pavilion then shook his head – it wasn't safe to assume Big Uncle was asleep. They waited, both of them nodding off at times, while Big Uncle tossed and turned above them. Finally, he was snoring and Kitchen Boy went to fetch the brazier. He had brought cloth pads to protect his hands from the hot earthenware and he carried the brazier with his good hand supporting the weight from underneath and his other hand holding it steady.

He peered through the bamboo slats of the pavilion to check Big Uncle's position, then he slipped under the floor to set up the brazier. Kancil followed him into the crawl space and watched while he got the *jamu* smoking. He used the palm leaf fan to direct the aroma up through the floor slats to Big Uncle's nose.

Kancil raised her head to speak through the floor, into Big Uncle's ear. "There was once a peaceful village in the heart of the Mataram lands," she began. She spoke in her best Jawa language and made her voice as deep as possible. She reasoned that Big Uncle would be more likely to believe his "vision" if it didn't have the voice of a young girl.

"The good Bapak Thani of the village had a loyal

wife and a beautiful daughter," she continued, avoiding Kitchen Boy's eye for fear she would start giggling. "He was a good and just Bapak Thani and when word came that a new prince would soon arrive to reclaim the region for the Majapahit Kingdom, he saw a chance to rid his village of the bandits that roamed the forest and goaded the volcano, Mbah Merapi, into vengeful acts of rage. Yet unbeknown to the good Bapak Thani, the prince was not what he seemed …"

Kancil kept talking, reciting the script she had been preparing in her head all afternoon. Her story laid bare the truth about the prince and the scoundrel and their plots to retrieve the gold and send the villagers to their deaths. "… Then a spirit spoke to the Bapak Thani in the night and in the morning he knew he must stop the wedding."

Kancil wasn't confident that Big Uncle would think of a way to stop the wedding and expose the bandits on his own. Yet, none of the village elders had struck her as particularly good at directing him either. Then she thought of the *dalang*. Could the puppet master direct Big Uncle as skilfully as he directed a shadow play? She remembered the way Dalang Mulyo had nodded to her that night before the *wayang* performance and decided she had to trust him.

"To find a way to expose the bandits he sought the

advice of the wise *dalang*," she finished, her voice hoarse.

Now she sat back on her heels and massaged her temples. Kitchen Boy kept fanning the smoke up through the bamboo slats until the last of the *jamu* was reduced to dust. He smothered the coals with a handful of dirt then eased over and put his lips to Kancil's ear. "He's not snoring," he whispered.

It was true. Kancil hadn't noticed; she was concentrating so hard on getting her story right. Was he awake? They sat silently for what seemed like forever, hardly daring to breathe, waiting. Finally, the floor creaked as Big Uncle rolled over. He started to snore. Kancil and Kitchen Boy both sighed with relief and didn't waste any time getting out from under the pavilion.

Kitchen Boy scooped up the brazier and darted down the dark path to dispose of the evidence down the kitchen drain. Kancil hobbled across the courtyard – the unnatural position she had held to talk through the floor was causing spasms to charge up and down her back. When she reached the shadows near the verandah she straightened up to ease the pain and there, stretched out on the verandah daybed, was Citra.

Their eyes met. Kancil's first instinct was to duck her head and scurry away but she stopped herself. Instead she held her cousin's gaze. "I told him the truth," she murmured. "It's up to him now." For a moment, Citra looked taken aback. Then she raised her chin to look down on her cousin with her usual haughty scowl before turning her back and lying down with her face to the wall.

Sleep would not come to Kancil that night. She lay staring into the blackness and when the blackness gave way to faint, pre-dawn outlines she gave up on sleep, rolled off the sleeping mat and went to the kitchen.

"Citra saw us," she murmured to Kitchen Boy when he came in with the rice.

"I know," he nodded. "Don't worry. You did everything you could do." He left the rice and walked towards the front of the house to join the men for the tiger hunt. Kancil felt let down. She wanted Kitchen Boy's reassurance but he seemed just as despondent as her.

Kancil had hulled the rice, lit the fire and swept the kitchen when she heard the sound of men chanting loudly and beating drums at the front of the house, making themselves brave with a big show of noise. She listened as they moved down the path to the north *pendopo* and beyond the north gate, leaving the village feeling eerily quiet.

Bibi arrived and for once, Kancil found her grumbling and stick-thumping comforting. If Citra had betrayed them, then Bibi would have been crowing.

"They expect a feast, of course," Bibi huffed, "to celebrate if they catch a tiger and to take their minds off their failure if they don't. So get to it, you lazy bint – those coconuts won't grate themselves. Now where's that girl of mine?"

She turned towards the kitchen door to yell for Ida but stopped in her tracks when, instead of Ida, she saw Citra.

"Bibi, I have a headache. Make me some ginger tea. I'll be in the pavilion," said Citra.

"Of course, Miss Citra," Bibi replied.

"Thank you," Citra said softly. She was looking at Kancil.

When Kancil took the ginger tea to her cousin in the pavilion, she found Mother there combing Big Aunt's hair and tweaking out the grey strands. Mother looked surprised to see her. Big Aunt looked like she could smell a bad smell.

"Massage my feet," said Citra as Kancil slipped the teapot and cup onto the pavilion floor.

Kancil kneeled on the step and took her cousin's feet in her lap. Mother was smiling down at her. Clearly she thought this was a great improvement in her daughter's status.

"Mother, when I'm married, will I be a princess?" Citra asked.

"You will be a highly respected lady," Big Aunt replied.

"But will I be a princess?"

"That will be up to the royal family to decide. The important thing is that you will be married to a prince."

"And is that prince married to anyone else?" Citra asked.

Big Aunt made an irritated noise in her throat. "You know the answer to that question. The princess died in childbirth."

"I know *that*. At least, I know what I've been *told* about that. That wasn't my question. I want to know about other *living* wives."

"Bah! Such a selfish girl, always thinking of yourself!" said Big Aunt. "That is not for you to wonder about. Your father has made a decision for the good of your family and your village. It is not your place to ask questions."

"We only have his word though, don't we?" Citra continued. "That he is who he says he is."

Big Aunt gasped at this. "He carries the Majapahit seal!" she exclaimed. "How dare you question a prince?"

Citra looked down at Kancil with an expression that said "I tried".

Kancil bowed her head so her cousin wouldn't see the

expression on her own face. It said "If that's the best you can do, then we're all doomed".

You should be grateful, she reminded herself. Citra believes you, and Big Uncle didn't throw you out of the village at dawn so either he believes you too or he slept through your performance. In any case, Kitchen Boy was right, you did what you could and now it's up to Citra and Big Uncle to stop the prince.

She *was* glad that her plan hadn't yet proved a failure. However, she couldn't help feeling disappointed that she hadn't thought of a way to get hold of the tiger stone, if indeed it even existed.

Her only chance of finding Agus now was to go to Pekalongan with the *dalang*'s troupe. Her plan had been to make herself indispensable to the *pesinden* singer so she would insist Dalang Mulyo took her with them, but she hadn't seen the performers since the night of the *wayang* performance. She doubted the *pesinden* singer even remembered what she looked like.

21

THE TIGER HUNTERS

The hunters returned in the late afternoon. Kancil was walking from the bathing pool when she heard the clang of Bibi's cane on the iron pot, calling her back to the kitchen. She quickly wrung the water from her hair and coiled it into a knot at the nape of her neck, ready for work.

"They want ginger tea," Bibi said when Kancil entered. "Use the good palm sugar." Two of the prince's men came to the kitchen. Between them they carried a pole with the carcass of a young *banteng* steer strung to it. Several dead birds were tied by their feet to one end of the pole and the glossy pelts of two weasels hung at the other end. Kancil was relieved to see no mouse deer on the pole – that, she was sure, would have been a very bad omen.

Bibi sniffed when she saw the meat. "No tiger then?" she asked.

"Sadly no, dear Bibi," Bapak Pohon chortled, as he followed the prince's men up the path with his butchering knife. "That *banteng* will make a tasty satay, though, and the prince was quite taken by the weasels' fur. Did you know that traders in Trowulan will pay a sack of rice for one pelt?"

"Hmpf," said Bibi, poking at the weasels with her stick. "Can't eat fur and they're scrawny little things." She took hold of one of the birds, a fat pigeon, and inspected it carefully. "The birds are all right," she admitted. "I guess there'll be enough without sending the boy out to collect some bats. Where is he, anyway?"

"Oh, he's about," Bapak Pohon said. He motioned to the men to hang the *banteng* steer on the butchering hook by the door.

So Kitchen Boy was all right. Though Kancil would have liked to be sure that "about" didn't mean tied up somewhere being punished for his part in last night's events. Despite Citra's reaction, Kancil wasn't confident that they had won Big Uncle over. There was no sign that the prince had fallen out of favour.

When Kancil reached Big Uncle's *pendopo* with the ginger tea, she found the prince seated on the heavy teak stool where Big Uncle usually sat. The parasol bearer sat behind him on the floor while Big Uncle and the other village elders were seated in a semicircle at the prince's feet. Kancil grew more despondent as she listened to the men's conversation. Any stiffness between the prince and her uncle had vanished. They joked together about the unsuccessful tiger hunt.

"I suppose it was a foolish idea," said the prince, "but I thank you all for humouring me. It is so rare that I have the opportunity to step down from my *jempana* and mix with ordinary people."

Kancil thought that Big Uncle would bristle at being called "ordinary". Instead, he inclined his head as though acknowledging a compliment. Kancil now hoped that Big Uncle *hadn't* heard her speaking the night before because if he had, he clearly hadn't believed her and was probably just waiting for the prince to leave so he could wring her neck without causing a scene.

"If you are troubled by tigers at the *joglo*, Your Highness," said Bapak Iya, "we can always lay a trap at night. It is the, er, more usual way of dealing with them here."

"Thank you, my friend. That really won't be necessary. It was the thrill of the chase that I craved. I have been so entranced by these inland forests and I thought a tiger would be a wonderful memento to take back to the capital. Never mind, I will be happy to settle for taking my beautiful bride with me."

An image of Citra trussed up on the hunters' pole flashed into Kancil's mind. She felt a stab of pity for her cousin.

"Which reminds me," the prince continued, "the, ahem, the wedding ..."

"Ah yes," said Big Uncle, "that is the reason I was a little delayed in joining you for the hunt this morning. I was making the final arrangements with the *dalang*. Here he is now."

Kancil followed Big Uncle's gaze and saw Dalang Mulyo walking towards them. Behind him in procession were the singer and the musicians with their *gamelan* instruments. Bringing up the rear was Kitchen Boy, who carried a pole across his shoulders, with four long bamboo *tuak* flasks strung from each end.

"Your Highness," said Dalang Mulyo, bowing deeply when he reached the step of the *pendopo*. "Forgive me for not accompanying you on the hunt today. I was practising all day with my musicians.

"Now, with your royal permission, my troupe requests the privilege of entertaining you this evening. We bring you this gift of *tuak* to thank you for the great honour of performing at your wedding celebration tomorrow." He spoke in such beautiful polite Jawa that all the men in the *pendopo* unconsciously sat up a little straighter.

"Of course, of course," said the prince. He motioned for Dalang Mulyo to join the men in the *pendopo*.

One of the musicians rolled out a mat on the ground and the others set up their instruments. Kitchen Boy stepped forwards and laid the *tuak* flasks on the *pendopo* floor. He laid one flask at a slight angle to the others and tapped it once before moving away.

"Allow me, Your Highness," said Big Uncle, taking the flask and pouring a large cup for the prince.

Kancil was called to the kitchen and as day turned to night she hurried back and forth carrying full and empty dishes. Each time she drew close to the front of the house the noise from the *pendopo* seemed a little louder and more soaked in laughter. The musicians added to the festive atmosphere and flashes of lightning from a storm brewing on the other side of the mountain gave the evening a sense of expectation.

Whenever Kancil approached the *pendopo* it seemed that Big Uncle was filling the prince's *tuak* cup. None of the village elders were saying much. They seemed to be enjoying listening to the prince and the *dalang* exchange anecdotes of their travels. The prince looked relaxed, sitting back in his chair and laughing between gulps of *tuak* as Dalang Mulyo told a tale, then sitting forwards and waving his arms to illustrate a bigger and better tale.

The prince's men under the tree also looked relaxed – Kitchen Boy had positioned himself nearby and was attentively refilling their *tuak* cups. The only person who appeared uncomfortable was the parasol bearer. He sat behind the prince's chair, tense and wary.

Villagers had gathered in the shadows to listen. Kancil wound through the crowd with a plate of crispy melinjo nut crackers, keeping one ear tuned to Dalang Mulyo. He was telling a story about performing at the wedding of a village elder's son just over the border in Sunda. "I had to concentrate so hard to remember to speak polite Sunda instead of polite Jawa that I found myself making the most simple mistakes."

There was a hush in the crowd and people looked at each other in confusion. Dalang Mulyo had slipped into speaking the marketplace dialect that the bandits used when they thought they were unobserved. The village elders in the *pendopo* continued to nod and smile, pretending that they understood. Kancil stood still. She knew now she had been right to trust the *dalang*.

"So you can imagine my embarrassment," the *dalang* continued, "when I realised I had referred to the village head man as the village coconut. It was an easy mistake to make – '*kelapa*' instead of '*kepala*' – but that only made it *more* embarrassing."

The prince roared with laughter and slapped his

thigh, oblivious to the trap that was being laid. The parasol bearer realised though and leaned forwards to warn him. It was too late.

"That's *nothing*," the prince replied in the same dialect. "There was this one time when I was in Muara Jati …" he stopped and looked around him, suddenly aware that the musicians had stopped playing and everyone was staring at him. "What?" he slurred.

"Ah, well," said the *dalang*, speaking everyday Jawa now, "I guess they're all wondering how a member of the Majapahit royal family comes to speak the language of thieves and tricksters with such ease."

The prince waved his hand dismissively. "I've been around," he said. He didn't seem to realise the trouble he was in. The parasol bearer sunk his head into his hands.

Big Uncle stood up, towering over the prince.

"How dare you!" the prince spluttered. "I am cousin of King Hayam Wuruk and you, you! A nobody from nowhere and yet you dare to raise your head above me?" He staggered to his feet and stood facing Big Uncle, hands on his hips. Slowly, all the other men in the *pendopo* raised themselves so they were standing in a circle around the prince. The prince reached behind him for his *kris* but the parasol bearer caught him by the wrist. Scar and the other bearers looked about in alarm – they were outnumbered.

"You may be the cousin of King Hayam Wuruk," said Big Uncle, "but you are not the Prince of Mataram. You seek only your own profit – as we would expect from a bandit – but you are a fool if you think the people of Prambanan will be drawn into your trap."

The prince swayed slightly, the reality of his situation starting to seep through the fuzz of *tuak*. "How did you know?" he asked.

"I had suspected you for some time," Big Uncle said loftily, "but I had no proof. Then last night I had a vision. Mbah Merapi sent the spirits to me to confirm my suspicions. Your big mistake, you see, was to anger Mbah Merapi by stealing the treasures from the forest temples all those years ago. The mountain is patient. He never forgets and he will always protect those who are loyal to him.

"You thought that you could deceive us and use us to fight your petty battle with your cousin then send us all to our deaths."

Kancil heard a cry of horror from behind the fence; it was Big Aunt. Citra had not made a sound.

Fat drops of rain began to fall and lightning lit up the sky.

"I am not such a fool," Big Uncle continued. "You and your men will leave this place and never return to Mataram. As I am a compassionate man, I will not send you out into this storm tonight." The time that passed between the rolls of thunder and flashes of lightning was getting shorter and shorter as the storm approached the village.

The musicians had quietly packed up their instruments and slipped into the courtyard to stow them under cover. The villagers, meanwhile, sought what shelter they could. Kancil caught sight of Kitchen Boy huddling under an umbrella leaf and went to join him.

Bapak Pohon and five other strong village men rounded up the bandits and were using sticks to prod them towards the *pendopo*.

"Tie them up," Big Uncle commanded. "You will stay under guard in the *pendopo* tonight. Tomorrow at first light you will be escorted to Salatiga where you will be handed over to the King's soldiers," he said to the prince, before turning to leave the *pendopo* with the other village elders and Dalang Mulyo.

"You'll never find the treasure," Scar snarled.

Big Uncle wavered slightly and turned back to speak. The *juru kunci* interrupted. "You cannot eat gold and it will not shelter you from the storm," he said. "Our treasure is the rice harvest and the gentle seasons that the spirits bestow upon us. The mountain has taken the gold and you bandits would be wise to accept that as your punishment and forget about your stolen treasure."

"What about the scoundrel?" Kancil whispered to Kitchen Boy. "Big Uncle didn't say anything about him."

Kitchen Boy shook his head. "Don't worry about the scoundrel," he said. "He's going to lead me to the treasure. You'd better get back to the kitchen. Bibi will be looking for you." The rain was falling in sheets now and the only villagers remaining were Bapak Pohon and his men standing guard around the *pendopo*.

"Are you crazy?" Kancil whispered. "He's out there with two of the bandits. It's far too dangerous. You heard the *juru kunci*, the treasure isn't important."

"And you heard the prince two nights ago tell them to keep their distance for five days. They won't know the prince's plan has come undone. I'll follow them to the hiding place then, when they go to the meeting place, I'll steal the treasure back. Don't you want to find the tiger stone?"

"Ye-es, but ..." Kancil didn't know what to say. Of course she wanted to find the tiger stone and she wanted to find Agus but what if the tiger stone was just a stone and Agus was dead, after all? "You're my only friend," she said. "I don't want you to get yourself killed for the sake of finding out if there was any truth in a holy man's story."

Kitchen Boy's face broke into a huge grin. He made a small bow. "I am honoured to be your friend," he said, "and I won't squander that friendship by getting myself killed. The scoundrel knows the forest well, but I know a few things he doesn't. Now stop worrying."

22

THE VANISHING

"It was you, wasn't it?" Mother whispered into the dark when Kancil reached the shack.

"Mmm," Kancil replied. She was thinking about Kitchen Boy. His confidence was going to get him into trouble one day. She hoped that day wasn't soon.

"You saved us," Mother whispered.

"Not yet," Kancil answered, "we're still here." Then she lay down and fell fast asleep.

When she woke, it was still night. She sat bolt upright. Mother was also sitting up and it took Kancil a moment to figure out that lightning had struck close by. Through the clatter of the storm, Kancil thought she heard men shouting at the front of the house, but it was difficult to be sure and her head was still fuzzy from sleep. She lay back down and let the sound of driving rain carry her off to sleep again.

Mother shook Kancil awake at dawn and she rushed to the kitchen to do her chores, expecting Kitchen Boy to be there with the rice ready for her to hull. He was nowhere to be seen. She lit the fire and swept the kitchen and waited. She could sense that something was wrong.

"The bandits have gone. There's to be a *selamatan* to thank the spirits for protecting us," Bibi said when she arrived. She banged her cane on the shelf where a cone-shaped basket sat. The basket was for shaping the *nasi tumpeng*, the yellow rice mountain that formed the centrepiece of a *selamatan* ceremony. "Get that down for me and give it a wipe," she said.

Kancil pointed towards the empty stool where Kitchen Boy usually sat.

"Gone with the bandits by the looks of it. Good riddance if you ask me," Bibi said. She spat into the dirt. Then she whacked Kancil on the side of the head with her cane. "Don't just stand there gaping, girl, get to work."

Ida arrived with the rice and the news. The bandits had accomplices. They had crept into the village during the storm and untied the men in the *pendopo*. When they realised what was happening, the guards had fought back but the bandits overpowered them. Lightning struck the *pendopo* and in the confusion, the bandits had disappeared. At first light the village men had gone looking for them but they had vanished without a trace. Kitchen Boy had been at the *pendopo* with the guards. Nobody could remember seeing him after the lightning strike.

"Hmpf," Bibi grunted, "they couldn't remember seeing him because that good-for-nothing foundling saw the opportunity to sneak away with those thieves to get his hands on some of their treasure. *Our* treasure, I should say. Bah! Bapak Thani is too kind-hearted, he should have marched them all into the river last night."

Kancil listened with a sinking heart. The scoundrel and the two other bandits must have disobeyed the prince's orders and been near enough to the village to know what had happened. Or perhaps they had a secret signal that she didn't know about.

She was certain that Kitchen Boy wouldn't have left the way Bibi described. That could only mean that he had been kidnapped by the bandits. She remembered what he had said once, that his freedom to come and go as he pleased meant that nobody would come looking for him if he disappeared. She also remembered promising him that she would look for him.

Some friend I am, she thought.

"Dalang Mulyo's going to leave after the *selamatan*," Ida added. "Ibu Thani said to prepare food for his journey."

"Typical," Bibi grumbled. "As if I haven't got enough to do already."

Kancil scooped rice into the hulling bowl and swung the pounding rod down on the grains. She might as well be one of those grains of rice, she thought, being pummelled by forces beyond her control. Her belief that the scoundrel and the treasure would lead her to Agus had just been wishful thinking. When the *dalang* and his troupe left, she would lose her only chance of escape and without Kitchen Boy to talk to she would be right back where she was when she first arrived here.

Listen to yourself! she thought crossly, full of self-pity because you're lonely when Kitchen Boy is probably being tortured at this very moment. That stopped her feeling sorry for herself, but it didn't make her feel any better.

The *juru kunci* placed an offering of rice cakes and flowers with a stick of burning incense under the spirit tree at the north temple gate. Big Aunt placed the *nasi tumpeng* in the middle of a mat that had been laid out under the tree and the village elders and Dalang Mulyo sat in a circle around the rice mountain. Bapak Pohon and the other guards, all looking rather battered and bruised, formed a circle around the elders and then the rest of the village men joined in. They all sat cross-legged with their eyes closed and palms upturned while the *juru kunci* muttered to the spirits, offering gratitude for being saved from the bandits and inviting them to join the villagers for a celebratory feast.

Kancil sat in the north *pendopo* with Mother, Bibi and Ida, behind Big Aunt and Citra. They were surrounded by pots of rice and stewed vegetables, platters of sweet cakes and a pile of banana leaf plates. The *selamatan* ceremony would end when the *juru kunci* broke the peak off the *nasi tumpeng* mountain. That would be the signal to Kancil to start serving offerings of food onto leaves and passing them forwards to Citra to hand out to every villager – the spirits would feed on the essence of the offerings while the physical food would fill the people's bellies.

The signal was given and Kancil began passing the plates forwards. Citra took them without turning around. Kancil stared resentfully at her cousin's back. She had been saved from her fate. The least she could do was give her a sign that she felt bad about Kitchen Boy. Everybody else was behaving as if he had never existed.

The last of the food was served, the mat was rolled up and the villagers drifted away to resume their afternoon chores, just like an ordinary day. Kancil was almost ready to believe she had dreamed the whole episode but Dalang Mulyo and his troupe were still there, a reminder that a world existed outside the village, and that Kancil's chance to join that world was slipping away.

She was standing on the path, about to carry a basket of leftovers back to the house, when she heard Big Uncle speak to the *dalang*. "Please wait until morning to start your journey. You don't want to be in the forest at nightfall, and you are, of course, welcome to stay."

Kancil thought of Kitchen Boy. Would he still be in the forest at nightfall or had he been carried far away? The bandits had probably found out about his role in protecting the village from tigers and decided he would be useful to keep close.

They wouldn't dare try to sell their gold in Salatiga – Bapak Iya had already sent his son to raise the alarm there. So they would want Kitchen Boy's help to carry their loot to the coast. Kancil didn't want to contemplate the alternative. She convinced herself that he would go along with them until they got to the port, then give them the slip.

Perhaps, she thought, he would team up with her brother. She tried to summon Agus into her mind, but he felt far away, as he always did, in the way that gave her comfort because it made her believe he was still alive.

Could that work with Kitchen Boy too?

She summoned him into her mind and there he was, standing right in front of her. Kancil's heart sank at the realisation that Kitchen Boy had met his fate. But no! He really was standing right in front of her. He was dirty, scratched and bruised and blood seeped from a makeshift bandage on his arm but he was alive and he was grinning at her like an idiot.

23

THE TIGER STONE

"It's the boy!" cried Ibu Tari. "Oh dear, he's hurt." Ibu Tari hurried over and helped Kitchen Boy to the *pendopo* while everybody else gaped at him. Kitchen Boy swayed slightly but he managed to walk to the *pendopo*. He was carrying something wrapped in an old *sarung*. It was the size of a jackfruit and he placed it carefully on the floor in front of Big Uncle. He eased himself up into the *pendopo* and bowed.

Big Uncle unwrapped the *sarung* to reveal a large, ornately decorated bowl. It was badly tarnished but there was no doubt that it was gold. Big Aunt gasped. "It's the holy water bowl that was stolen from the temple," she said.

Everybody looked at Kitchen Boy, waiting for an explanation. "Drink?" he whispered hoarsely. Kancil was already on her way. She dashed over to a clump of coconut trees near the *pendopo*. The pile of young coconuts that was always kept under the trees had been diminished by all the feasting of late but there were still a few. She took a large knife that Bibi had brought from the kitchen and with three sharp blows took the top off a coconut.

Kitchen Boy drank the juice in a few gulps and smacked his lips.

"Well?" said Big Uncle.

"I followed them from the *pendopo*," said Kitchen Boy with a shrug. "The temple treasures are all buried in jars in a cave. This one was all I could carry but the rest of the gold is quite safe. Really, we owe the bandits gratitude for burying the gold in the first place. They chose a place that was safe from Mbah Merapi's wrath, much safer than the temple."

"But the bandits," Big Uncle said, "where are they? How do we know the treasure is safe? You can't expect us to believe that you fought them all off single-handed!"

Kitchen Boy sighed. "Forgive me for speaking bluntly, Bapak Thani," he said, "but tell me – when your sister brought me to you and told you that she had found me with a tigress, you didn't believe her, did you? You thought I was her fatherless child and she made up a fanciful story to save face."

Kancil followed Kitchen Boy's gaze and was surprised to see Small Aunt standing next to Mother. She looked cross. Big Uncle glowered at Kitchen Boy. He said nothing.

Kitchen Boy let the silence stretch to an uncomfortable length before he continued. "Well," he said, "you should have believed her. Luckily for us (not so luckily for the bandits) they buried their treasure in the very cave where your sister found me all those years ago — a cave that a certain family of tigers considers to be their private property."

He looked up at Small Aunt. "Do you think it's time they knew the truth?" he asked.

She shrugged. "As you wish," she said. "The holy woman I serve, the woman who was the daughter of the old Bhre. She is the boy's mother. She told me where to find him but she is silent on the identity of his father and why she chose to leave him in the care of tigers."

I was right! Kancil thought, remembering the day she had sat under the banyan tree with Kitchen Boy. I wonder if he always knew or if my curiosity made him ask questions.

"So it looks like I'm the closest thing to Majapahit royalty that this village has seen for many a year," Kitchen Boy said. Big Aunt was making horrified choking noises. "Don't worry," he continued, "I have no desire to marry your daughter."

He turned back towards Big Uncle. "Trust me, the treasure is safe where it is, and I wouldn't recommend anyone try to retrieve it without my help. And no, I didn't fight the bandits off by myself, but they won't be troubling you again."

Big Uncle picked up the golden bowl and inspected it closely. Intricate scenes of gods and demons were carved into the outer surface and the lip and foot of the bowl were trimmed with golden rope. He passed the bowl to Ki Sardu, the priest, who gazed at it in a rapture.

"We should bury it again," the priest said. Everybody looked at him in surprise.

"Ki Sardu is right," said the *juru kunci*. "The gods have abandoned the forest temples. The treasure is not safe there until they return, and the tigers have proven themselves to be good guardians. They will give us a signal when it is safe to retrieve it."

Kitchen Boy bowed respectfully to the *juru kunci*. "I can take you there tomorrow," he said. Then he spoke to Dalang Mulyo. "Sir, is it true that you will leave tomorrow, making for the port of Pekalongan?"

Dalang Mulyo nodded.

"Bapak Thani," Kitchen Boy said, addressing Big Uncle again. "I humbly beg that as a reward for my part in ridding the village of the bandit scourge, I be released to follow Dalang Mulyo and his troupe. I believe the *dalang* is in need of an apprentice."

Dalang Mulyo looked a little surprised then he smiled and shrugged his shoulders as if to say, "Why not?"

Kancil felt faint. Was Kitchen Boy weaving a clever plan to help her escape or was he going to abandon her? Big Uncle had the look of a man accustomed to being in control, watching the power slip from his grasp. He looked towards Big Aunt in confusion. She was glaring at Kitchen Boy, her mouth turned down in distaste.

"Your services will be required when it is time to retrieve the treasure," Big Uncle said.

"Tigers have no use for gold," the *juru kunci* said slowly, "and nor do humble villagers. The tigers will protect the treasure until the gods require it and Mbah Merapi will reward us for not succumbing to greed as the bandits did."

"So it would appear that I'm not really needed after all — once I've helped bury this bowl again tomorrow morning," said Kitchen Boy.

Big Uncle waved his hand dismissively. "Go then," he said, "you won't be missed."

"There is one other thing," said Kitchen Boy, retrieving a small cloth-wrapped parcel that was rolled into the waist of his *sarung*. "I found this."

He placed the cloth before Big Uncle who unwrapped

it to reveal a pendant made of polished stone. The stone was striped with bands of golden and chocolate brown that shimmered like layers of light. The pendant was set in a thin silver frame that hung from a string made of knotted twine.

The village elders all inspected the pendant closely. The priest shook his head. "This is not from the forest temple," he said.

"Was it buried with the treasure?" Big Uncle demanded.

Kitchen Boy leaned his head to one side; he seemed to be choosing his words carefully. "It was ... nearby," he said. "It ... ahem ... it is, of course, up to the village elders to decide what happens to it, but I had a strong feeling when I picked it up that it should go to the kitchen girl."

The *juru kunci*, who was inspecting the pendant, looked at Kancil thoughtfully. Before he had a chance to speak, Big Uncle took the pendant from his hand.

"No!" Big Uncle said. "My daughter suffered the most from that impostor. She should be the one to receive this gift. My dear ..." he turned to Citra who was sitting beside him and handed her the pendant. Kancil saw Kitchen Boy's face fall.

Citra hooked a finger through the loop at one end of the necklace and held the pendant up to the light.

"Today was to be my wedding day and you promised me gold," she said. "This isn't gold, it's a trick of the light. Anyway, it's broken." She held up the other end of the necklace, which was frayed – there was nothing to fit through the loop, to clasp it round the wearer's neck. "You might as well let her have it." She leaned forwards to drop the pendant on the floor in front of Kancil. As she sat back she caught Kancil's eye. She smiled.

Dalang Mulyo reached over and picked up the pendant. "You're the girl who doesn't speak, aren't you?" he said to Kancil. She looked up at him and nodded.

"It's true this pendant is not made of gold," he continued. "But this stone has come from far away and I do believe that it might have the power to lift the curse of silence that has befallen you." His face was serious but there was a twinkle in his eye. Was it possible he had overheard her talking to Kitchen Boy?

"And you know," the *dalang* added, "I think I have the very thing to fix the clasp." He took a small bag from his luggage and began searching its many pockets and pouches. "A boy I met on the road from Bubat gave it to me in exchange for food – said it was a lucky charm. Funny thing is, he had eyes like yours. I knew there was someone you reminded me of. Ah, there it is." He held up a tiny cowry shell, then turned to the singer, handing her the shell and the necklace. "My dear, you have much nimbler fingers than me," he said.

The singer carefully tied the frayed end through the shell then handed the necklace to Kancil.

It might just be an ordinary stone, Kancil reminded herself, preparing for disappointment. She was scared, too. If the stone did have some kind of power, what would it do to her? Would she know how to control it? She held Kitchen Boy's gaze for reassurance. He was transfixed, his mouth open in expectation. Clearly he didn't think it was an ordinary stone.

Suddenly, Kancil felt incredibly calm. She could sense her father sitting beside her, encouraging her to be brave. She took a deep breath.

As the stone touched Kancil's chest and she slipped the shell through the loop at the back of her neck, a strange sensation overcame her. For a moment she couldn't focus and she panicked as she felt as though she was being sucked under water. Then her vision cleared. She was still sitting in the *pendopo*, looking at Kitchen Boy, and at the same time she was floating, watching a different scene. She could see Agus. He was at the port of Pekalongan, negotiating a passage back to Sunda on a trading ship. "Wait!" she told him in her mind. "Wait for me!" She saw him look up, a puzzled expression on his face; then he shook his head at the ship's captain and walked away.

At the same time, Kancil sensed her father walking away from her. She didn't try to stop him. She knew it was time for him to go.

"Look at her eyes," said the singer. "Have they always had those gold flecks?"

Kancil felt the colour rising to her cheeks; she didn't like everybody staring at her. She looked down at her hands. Be brave, she told herself.

"Well, say something, girl," Dalang Mulyo said. "Don't make a liar of me."

Kancil looked up. "My name–" she began. Her voice sounded thin and weak. She cleared her throat and squared her shoulders, then in a clear strong voice she said, "My name is Kancil. I am from Sunda and I am *not* bandit spawn." She turned to Big Uncle and bowed deeply. "Thank you for protecting me when I needed your help. I trust my mother has a home here should she choose to stay. But I must leave you now. My brother is waiting for me in Pekalongan."

NOW

EPILOGUE

"Selokan, Selokan, Selokan." The bus conductor hung from the door, calling out the destination as the minibus swung round the corner. When he saw Aryani step from the curb he tapped on the roof to alert the driver, who slowed down ever so slightly. Aryani leaped onto the bus. She had been in Yogyakarta for three months now and she was starting to feel at home, though getting on and off buses that never came to a complete halt was still a challenge.

She let out a long sigh as she sat down on the cracked vinyl seat next to Dwi, who lived at the same boarding house as Aryani but went to a different school.

"What's up with you, Ani?" Dwi asked.

Aryani shrugged. "I don't know," she said, "I just feel … weird." She had woken at three that morning with a feeling in her stomach that had been coming back at her in waves all day – a combination of pre-exam anxiety and homesickness. She couldn't figure out why, because her exams were ages away and she sometimes felt guilty about how much she *didn't* miss the village. "It must be something I ate," she said.

"There's someone to see you, Ani," said Bu Erma, the landlady, when Aryani and Dwi arrived home. She nodded towards the front room.

Sitting on the worn-out lounge chair was Bapak Surya, the neighbour who had brought Aryani to Yogyakarta. Her heart sank.

"I'm sorry, Ani," he said. He didn't need to tell her that Grandma was dead; her stomach told her that.

I should have known that was it, she thought. Why do I feel scared, though, like I'm about to sit a test?

"You'll have to pack quickly," Bapak Surya said. "We need to be at the bus terminal in half an hour."

Back in her room, Aryani changed out of her school uniform and threw some clothes into an overnight bag. She was about to shut the wardrobe when she remembered – the pendant. Her hand searched for the little cloth bag she had hidden at the back of the top shelf. The bag was hot, as though it had been lying in the sun, and the anxious feeling in her stomach was so bad that she thought she might be physically sick.

What had Grandma given her?

She slipped the pendant out of its bag and stuffed it into her jeans pocket then dashed to the shared bathroom. The nausea passed and she splashed water onto her face and wrists. There was nothing for it but to put the pendant on and see what happened. Aryani was certain that something *would* happen – for some reason it felt perfectly natural that Grandma would have given her something magical. She could remember Grandma's exact words: "You mustn't wear the necklace until I am gone. When you do, you will understand."

Aryani lifted the humble twine necklace to her throat and slipped the shell through the loop at the back of her neck. The sound of rushing water roared in her ears and she gasped for breath, her vision blurred. As the noise subsided, her vision cleared and she was looking at herself in the mirror again. She could feel Grandma's presence and there were others with her too. It was true, she *did* understand, though she couldn't explain the feeling if she tried.

A wave of giddiness washed over her. Aryani gripped the basin to steady herself and closed her eyes. Suddenly, she was in a forest. There were people around her, watching a boy walk towards a narrow gap in an embankment. It was the mouth of a shallow cave, where three earthenware jars had been wedged. The boy was carrying something in his arms. As he reached down to remove the lid of one jar and place the object inside, Aryani saw a flash of gold.

A movement in the forest above the embankment caught her eye. A tiger! Aryani sensed the people around her draw back in fear. The beast could easily pounce and pin her to the ground but Aryani felt no fear. The boy also seemed unconcerned. He dipped his head in greeting to the tiger and the tiger settled back on its haunches. On guard.

The boy turned around and grinned at Aryani. He looked so familiar, but who was he?

Aryani realised she had been holding her breath. She gasped for air and the forest scene dissolved as her eyes flew open.

She leaned over the sink and rested her forehead against the cool glass of the mirror, holding her own gaze.

Strange, she thought, I've never noticed those gold flecks in my eyes before.

As she straightened up, she realised she wasn't looking at herself any more; she was watching another scene unfold. The scene wasn't a forest, it was an open field. Nevertheless, she was sure it was the same place where the boy and the tiger had been, separated in time by many centuries. It felt like she was watching a live broadcast on television but she was the camera.

A small group of villagers was hurrying across the field towards a deep trench where five workers were waiting for them. The man leading the villagers had muddy legs and wore the same checked *sarung* and white singlet as the other workers. He was talking with great excitement to a man wearing the khaki uniform of a village official.

"We've been digging the irrigation channel for Nyonya Cipto for days," the man said, waving towards the trench. "Last night, as we were about to knock off, Witomoharjo's hoe hit something hard. We thought that we'd hit rock, and that we'd be here for weeks. But when we came back this morning and started digging again we realised it's not rock. It's … it's … something amazing!"

Aryani knew what the workers had found. Kitchen Boy's tiger spirits had protected the treasure for centuries. Why had they chosen this day, the day she received the tiger stone, to leave their post?

"Ani, are you all right?" Dwi's voice calling from the other side of the bathroom door broke the spell and Aryani was looking at herself in the mirror again.

"I'm fine," she called back. "Just … just a little upset."

"I heard about your grandma," Dwi said. "I'm sorry for your loss. Is there something I can do? Can I help you pack?"

Aryani stood up straight and brushed her fringe away from her eyes. She slipped the pendant out of sight inside the neck of her T-shirt. "No thanks, Dwi," she said. "I have everything I need."

GLOSSARY

Banteng: A breed of cattle native to South East Asia.

Bapak: Literally "father", a polite term of address for an adult man.

Beras kencur: A *jamu* tonic for tiredness, usually made from *kencur* root, raw rice, tamarind and sugar.

Bhre: Term of address for the ruler of a region in the Majapahit Kingdom.

Dalang: The puppet master who acts out the *wayang* shadow puppet play and conducts the *gamelan* orchestra.

Dalem: The enclosed back section of a *joglo* that serves as the private quarters.

Gamelan: A traditional percussion orchestra consisting of gongs, kettles and xylophone-like instruments.

Ibu: Literally "mother", a polite term of address for an adult woman.

Jamu: Herbal medicine.

Jempana: A covered litter (palanquin) carried on poles on the shoulders of four or more bearers.

Joglo: A traditional style of building with a steep roof held up by thick pillars. A *joglo* building usually has a deep verandah (*pendopo*) at the front and an enclosed space (*dalem*) at the back.

Juru kunci: Literally "master of the key", the *juru kunci* is custodian of a sacred place. The *Juru kunci* Merapi is custodian of Mount Merapi, the volcano near Yogyakarta.

Kain and **kemben**: A *kain* is a length of cloth. In Javanese traditional dress, women wear a three-metre-long *kain* wrapped around the body from the waist down (in English, a "sarong" but see *sarung* below). The *kain* may be secured by a *kemben*, a very long strip of cloth wrapped around the body like a bandage from hip to armpit. The long-sleeved *kebaya* blouse, worn over the top of the *kemben*, became part of traditional dress after the time in which this story is set.

Kangkung: A leafy green vegetable that grows in or near water (water spinach).

Kayu putih: Literally "white wood". *Kayu putih* oil is similar to ti-tree oil and eucalyptus oil. It is rubbed on the body or inhaled to treat everything from headaches to arthritis pain to travel sickness.

Kencur: The root of a type of lily used in *jamu* preparations.

Kendi: A flask with a spout for holding drinking water. Usually made from earthenware.

Kentongan: A length of bamboo or hollowed-out teak wood, usually hung in a central place in the village. Different rhythms are struck on the *kentongan* with a stick to signal alarm, village meetings etc.

Ki: A man with religious authority.

Kris: A double-edged dagger with a wavy blade. Traditionally a nobleman would wear a *kris* in the back of his belt.

Lontar: A type of palm leaf. Strips of *lontar* leaf, sewn together in a concertina arrangement, were used for writing on before the introduction of paper in Java.

Mbah: Literally "grandfather" (Javanese), a polite term of address for an old man. "Mbah Merapi" means "Fiery Grandfather".

Nasi tumpeng: A dish of yellow rice moulded into a cone shape and served at a *selamatan*.

Pendopo: A large, stand-alone open structure consisting of a roof held up by tall pillars, or a very deep verandah attached to the front of a building (see *joglo*). Used as a meeting place or for receiving guests, for ceremonies and community activities such as *gamelan* orchestra and dancing.

Pesinden: A female singer with the *gamelan* orchestra.

Pondok: A simple shack, often in a field or in the forest, for shelter against the elements.

Sarung: A "sarong" made from a tube of cloth wrapped

around the body and rolled at the waist to hold it in place. Traditionally, men wear *sarung* while women wear *kain*. A *sarung* can also be used as a footless sleeping bag.

Selamatan: A communal ritual feast to symbolise unity in the neighbourhood at the time of a significant event. From "*selamat*" meaning "safe from trouble".

Tuak: An alcoholic drink made from fermented palm sap or rice.

Wayang: A shadow puppet performance.

HISTORICAL NOTES

The characters and events in this story are fictional but the story is set in a real time and place: Java in the middle of the fourteenth century.

The Battle of Bubat, in which Kancil's father was killed, was a real event that occurred in 1279, according to the Javanese Saka calendar (1357 in the Western calendar). King Hayam Wuruk, the Majapahit King, was supposed to marry Princess Pitaloka, daughter of the King of Sunda. However, politics intervened and when the Sunda royal family reached Bubat, on their way to Trowulan, the capital, they were killed by Majapahit forces.

The forest temples near the village in this story are real temples – the Prambanan temple complex in Central Java near the city of Yogyakarta. The temples were built in the ninth century.

The civilisation that built the temples mysteriously vanished in the tenth century. There is evidence of a huge volcanic eruption at around this time, which might explain the sudden end to a thriving civilisation.

The story Kitchen Boy tells about the prince who turned the princess to stone is a well-known legend about the construction of the Prambanan temples.

If people continued to live in the shadow of Mount Merapi into the fourteenth century, they have left no trace. However, there is also no evidence that people *didn't* continue to live there. To this day, the fertile volcanic soil has convinced farmers to take their chances with the mountain although the authorities would prefer they moved permanently to safer ground. Local people still call the mountain Mbah Merapi, Fiery Grandfather, and they still turn to the *juru kunci* for advice on when to stay and when to go when Mbah Merapi gets angry.

The golden temple bowl and the other temple treasures are real. In October 1990, workers were digging an irrigation ditch in a rice field in Wonoboyo, Klaten – not far from the Prambanan temples. They uncovered three earthenware jars buried deep in the ground. When they opened them they found gold and silver treasures, including the temple bowl decorated with scenes from the Ramayana described in this story. The Wonoboyo Hoard, as it is known, is now on permanent display in the Treasure Room of the National Museum of Indonesia, in Jakarta. Historians believe it came from the Prambanan temples, though why and when it was buried remains a mystery.

ABOUT THE AUTHOR

Deryn Mansell has been fascinated by the history of Java ever since she visited Yogyakarta as a seventeen year old and experienced first-hand the majestic Prambanan and Borobudur temples. That visit motivated her to continue studying Indonesian and she has returned to Java many times since as a student, as a teacher and as a traveller.

In her working life, Deryn has been a teacher of Indonesian in Australia, a teacher of English in Indonesia, a researcher of language and intercultural communication and a coordinator of Asia literate business-people volunteering in Australian schools.

To find out more about the history and culture that inspired *Tiger Stone* visit derynmansell.com/tigerstone

ACKNOWLEDGEMENTS

First and foremost, thanks to Paul Mortensen, who kept me going and fed me *lahir dan batin*. Clare Renner and my classmates in the YA fiction class at RMIT gave me initial encouragement to pursue this story. Many friends and family members offered encouragement along the way, asked how the novel was going (or didn't ask – which was sometimes for the best), and offered constructive criticism of drafts – special thanks go to readers Abigail, Hannah and Rosie. Bagus and Pitaya were extremely generous with their time in Yogyakarta and shared their knowledge of temple sites, traditional architecture and village life. Ari and Dina provided valuable advice and feedback on my research into the history of Java and were patient with my angst over what to call people. Any errors of fact are, of course, my own responsibility. Thanks to Black Dog Books/Walker Books for taking a punt on a new author – especially to Maryann Ballantyne and Nicola Robinson. Last but not least, thank you for reading to the very last page.

MORE GREAT FICTION

ISBN 9781742032450   ISBN 9781742032467   ISBN 9781742032474

ISBN 9781922179210   ISBN 9781922179579

PRAISE FOR THE DRAGONKEEPER SERIES

"An enchanting blend of fantasy and history." **THE AGE**

"... proof that the fantasy genre is still working its magic."
JODIE MINUS, THE WEEKEND AUSTRALIAN

dragonkeeper.com.au